Will   Irma   Taranee   Cornelia   Hay Lin

The Return of a Queen

Adapted by ELIZABETH LENHARD

HarperCollins *Children's Books*

This book was first published in the USA in 2004 by Volo/Hyperion Books for Children
First published in Great Britain in 2005 by HarperCollins *Children's Books*, a division of
HarperCollins Publishers Ltd.

© 2006 Disney Enterprises, Inc.

ISBN 13 978-0-00-720947-7
ISBN 0-00-720947-9

1 3 5 7 9 10 8 6 4 2

The HarperCollins website is:
www.harpercollinschildrensbooks.co.uk

Visit www.clubwitch.co.uk

Printed and bound in Italy

MERIDIAN.
JUST A LITTLE WHILE AGO,
THIS CITY FELT THE WRATH
OF PHOBOS.

THE PRINCE OF METAMOOR
FORCED HIS SUBJECTS TO
LOOK INTO THE DEPTHS OF
HIS BLACK HEART . . .

. . . AND WHAT THEY SAW
WAS HORRIFYING.

PHOBOS'S HEART WAS A
DARK, EMPTY PLACE.

THOOM
THOOM
THOOM

BOOOM

ONE

In a dank chamber underneath the city of Meridian, Elyon pulled her brown cloak tightly around her skinny shoulders. The Guardians were standing in a circle around their friend, gazing at her.

Will, Taranee, Cornelia, Hay Lin, and Irma wore outfits suitable for superheroes, complete with fluttering wings.

It was hard to believe that, on an ordinary day, these girls wore jeans, sneakers, and fleece jackets. Their bodies were not as curvy and maybe even a little awkward. Their biggest problems were curfews, pop quizzes, and crushes.

The recent events of Elyon's life bubbled up in her mind. The saga was more outlandish than any fairy tale she'd read as a child.

Those stories are way plausible when you compare them to mine, she thought. For starters, I'm a princess. And not some ordinary pretty girl with a crown and servants: I'm the Light of Meridian, destined one day to rule over that city. Like most royals, I've got enemies, but mine come from the most unexpected place – my own family. My brother, also known as Prince Phobos, has plotted against me ever since I was a baby. Before he could do anything, though, three saviours took me away. Two of them became my adoptive parents and the third became Mrs. Rudolph, a lady who taught math at my school, the Sheffield Institute.

Together, Elyon mused, the three of them made sure that I grew up like an ordinary girl in the quiet town of Heatherfield. I passed notes in school and crushed on boys and drew hundreds of pictures and went to school dances. But that whole time, Phobos was looking for me. Without the Veil between Metamoor and the earth, he would have found me a lot sooner.

Luckily, the Veil *was* there – an invisible barrier that kept the baddies out of Heatherfield while keeping the good people of Heatherfield in the dark about all the teeming life just outside their universe.

The system had worked perfectly until the millennium struck. Fissures began opening in the Veil. Those holes – twelve of them – became portals that led straight from Metamoor to Heatherfield.

That's how Cedric slipped into town, told me about my true identity, and snatched me away to Meridian, Elyon reflected. But I wasn't the only one whose life got turned upside down that day.

Elyon emerged from her daydream briefly to gaze with sympathetic affection at her friends. Their collective path was very different from her own. The Guardians, too, had undergone massive transformations, thanks to the Oracle of Candracar.

Centuries ago, the Oracle had looked out upon the universe from his temple, which was perched somewhere in the heart of infinity. What he had seen worried him. He'd seen evil brewing in Metamoor, and so, he'd created the Veil to protect the earth.

Throughout time, the Oracle had appointed Guardians to protect the Veil. The Guardians he had most recently chosen were Will, Irma,

Taranee, Cornelia, and Hay Lin, whose names handily formed the acronym W.I.T.C.H. Besides giving them fluttery wings and beautiful, grown-up guises, the Oracle had infused them with the power of the elements.

Cornelia, serious, grounded, and as tall and slim as a graceful tree, had powers over the earth. Shooting green wisps of magic from her fingertips, she could blow a hole in a brick wall, set off an earthquake, or make a parched field erupt into wildflowers.

Irma was the group's water baby, summoning rain showers or ocean waves, or conjuring air bubbles to keep her friends afloat when they found themselves stranded in water – which happened far too often!

Hay Lin was in control of air, and Taranee was the Guardian in charge of fire.

And Will? When Elyon first met her, she'd been a shy girl who'd arrived in Heatherfield just before W.I.T.C.H. was formed. Yet the Oracle had made Will the group's leader. Within her body, she harbored a crystal orb that contained the Heart of Candracar. When the girls were in trouble, the glowing amulet emerged from Will's palm, infusing each

Guardian with maximum power.

For a long time, Will was uncomfortable running the show. The role of group leader had made her unsure and edgy. She hadn't known how to handle the large responsibility. But Will was finally becoming secure with her position and was taking charge with greater ease.

It must have been even harder for Cornelia to adjust, Elyon thought, stifling a little giggle.

If anyone knew about Cornelia's type A, "I'm in charge here" personality, it was Elyon. When they both lived in Heatherfield, the two girls had been best friends.

That meant that Cornelia was hit the hardest when I defected to Metamoor, Elyon thought with a guilty pang. It happened after Cedric convinced me that my adoptive parents weren't my parents at all, but traitors who'd kept me from my "loving brother."

This, Elyon thought, gazing at the group of fugitives huddled around her, is ample proof that what Cedric said was all a lie.

Phobos had spent years stealing Metamoor's magical energy in order to create a lavish palace for himself. He turned Meridian into an impoverished, dark place, and he oppressed his citizens until they were hungry, bitter, and constantly fearful of their ruler's wrath.

Not *everyone* had been cowed, though. Some of Phobos's flunkies had rebelled against him. The big, blue, bearish creature Vathek, for instance, had once terrorized the Guardians in the name of Phobos. Eventually, though, Vathek had seen Phobos for the deceitful villain that he was and joined the rebel forces led by Caleb.

Caleb. Elyon suppressed the quick sob that rose in her throat at the thought of the young rebel leader. He had undergone many transformations. Once, he had been just a flower. Then Phobos had turned him into a Murmurer, one of the slithery, rainbow- coloured creatures who saw and heard everything that happened in Meridian.

Most of the Murmurers remained mindlessly devoted spies. But Caleb had emerged from his servile trance, horrified by what he saw. That was when he'd changed yet again – from servant to rebel. Rejecting his former master, he'd thrown himself into the hero's life. And then one day he'd rescued Cornelia, when she'd gotten trapped in a watery portal. The moment the rebel and the Guardian had seen each other, they'd fallen in love.

Any weaker being might have disguised himself as a human and come to Heatherfield to enjoy the comforts of the earth, to be a normal teenager, to date a girl. Caleb, though, had had far too much honor to bail on his fellow Metamoorians. Not only had he decided to stay in Meridian, he had organised a troop of rebels to try to take back their world from Phobos's destructive grip.

For Caleb, the fight hadn't lasted long. After Phobos had tried – and failed – to steal Elyon's magic by crowning her with a dangerous head-piece, the rebels had risen up and waged war against the prince.

Phobos had been ready, with an army of lethal fighters called Annihilators, who looked like giant, indestructible turtles. They had zapped Metamoorians with their eye lasers. They'd stomped others under their feet and crushed others with their bare claws. Those whom the Annihilators missed, Phobos himself destroyed.

Caleb had been one of the prince's victims. Phobos had changed the beautiful young man one last time, turning him back into a glowing white flower, which Cornelia now held in her hand.

As Elyon looked around at the rebels there to support her reign, she realised she had never felt smaller or more scared.

At the moment, Will wasn't helping matters. As she stepped toward Elyon, her face was sympathetic, but determined. "We've got to do something," Will announced dramatically. Then she flung her arm out and pointed at the small crowd of Metamoorians gathered around them.

"These people are expecting something from us," Will reminded Elyon. "Especially from you."

Taranee stepped up behind Elyon and added, "You're their princess now."

Elyon looked miserably down at her feet. "A princess," she said, choking on the words, "without a throne."

"But one with great powers!" said a voice from the crowd.

Elyon gasped and looked up. That voice!

She'd have known it anywhere.

Instinctively, Elyon scanned the crowd for a redheaded woman. A human lady with a long, slender neck and sweet, slightly tired eyes.

Elyon was looking for her mum.

Elyon searched in vain through the sea of green, blue, and orange faces. Finally, a green-and-yellow-skinned creature emerged from the crowd with a smile that was very familiar. Elyon grinned.

Her adoptive mother no longer inhabited her gentle, redheaded human form. The way she looked now reflected her true identity. And the vermilion-and-green-skinned man with the floppy, pointed ears and long, yellow claws standing next to her was Elyon's father.

For a moment, Elyon's heart sank. This was not exactly the reunion she had envisioned.

Quickly, though, she smiled. It didn't matter what these people looked like. Elyon could see it in their eyes. They were . . .

"Mum! Dad!" Elyon cried.

"Oh, Elyon," the woman sobbed. "At last! We're together again!"

Later, Elyon wouldn't be able to recall how she'd made it across the crowded stone walkway into her parents' arms. She might have flown, for all she knew. All that mattered was that she had made it. She sank into her father's familiar bear hug and felt her mother's fluttery fingers stroking her hair.

As Elyon snuggled against her dad's rough cloak, she overheard Irma, joking as usual.

"I see a bit of resemblance, don't you?" she giggled.

"Don't be silly," Taranee replied. "Those are her adoptive parents, remember? The ones who took her away from here."

The words sounded strange to Elyon.

These blue-haired, colourful Metamoorians weren't even human. Yet Elyon knew it in her bones – they were her true family.

"After such a long time," Elyon said, placing her small hands into her mother's scaly ones, "I still don't know what to call you."

"You knew us as Thomas and Eleanor," Elyon's adoptive father said with a happy nod, "but my real name is Alborn. I was commander of the royal guard of Meridian."

"And I'm Miriadel," Elyon's adoptive mother said. "I was a captain in the army."

"So," Will interrupted, observing the warm

family's reunion with wide, excited eyes, "*you* can help us organise our defense against Phobos's soldiers!"

Elyon smiled. Royal destiny or no, she thought, it'd be nice to have a *little* guidance from a mum and dad again!

Alborn, however, looked hesitant. "I don't know," he said quietly. "How could we ever – "

"Please!" someone bellowed in a gravelly voice. Looking up, Elyon saw Vathek emerge from the crowd of Metamoorians.

"These people," he insisted to Alborn, "are ready to do anything you ask of them."

"Vathek's right," a pointy-eared man piped up. "We have to fight the tyrant. If we don't let our voices be heard now, then we deserve to be condemned to silence."

Alborn cocked his head in thought. The small motion brought nostalgic tears to Elyon's eyes. How many times had she seen her dad – in his human form – make that very same gesture at the dinner table in Heatherfield? It was such a familiar gesture that, for a moment, Elyon forgot where she was. She felt herself sinking into memories of her old life in Heatherfield. Alborn's next words jolted her out of her reverie and made her gasp.

"So be it," Alborn declared to the crowd. "We will fight. The key to our ultimate victory lies in the Crown of Light."

"If Elyon is to battle Phobos," Miriadel said with a nod, "she'll need her full powers, which means she'll have to be wearing the crown. But the crown is in Phobos's palace now."

That figures, Elyon thought darkly. Phobos kept it after he used it to try to destroy me! Luckily, my magical double took the fall for me. If only she could have hung on to the crown for me, too!

Taranee, for one, didn't seem fazed. She stepped forward, ready for action.

"So, what's the problem?" she asked Miriadel. "All we need to do is go to the palace and take the crown away from Phobos."

"Yes!" called an emerald-skinned man from the crowd. "To the palace!"

"To the palace!" echoed a dozen of his comrades. "To the palace!"

The mob was already beginning to surge toward the exit when Alborn held up his green hand.

"Calm down, friends," he called. "I'm afraid

it won't be so easy! All of our enthusiasm will do little against the prince's soldiers, much less those Annihilators."

"Alborn is right," Vathek said. He lumbered to the centre of the loose circle that the Metamoorians had formed.

"What we need," he continued, "is a surprise attack."

"Well put, Vathek," Elyon heard Miriadel say. "We have to surprise our foes in the streets of Meridian."

"We need to distract and divide them," Alborn added. His voice was strong and steady as he announced his plan. "It's the only way they can be weakened. We'll lure them away from the palace. And when they're all busy tracking us down, a small group of us will slip inside."

Elyon noticed a flash of purple out of the corner of her eye. Irma had trotted over to Hay Lin to murmur something in her ear. Back at Sheffield, Irma had never been a subtle sneak, and she definitely wasn't one now. Elyon overheard Irma's every word.

"They're going to put us right into the middle of this," she predicted fearfully. "Act as if nothing is happening, Hay Lin. Pretend you're not here!"

Hay Lin might have agreed with Irma's suggestion, but Will was having none of it. She stepped toward Elyon's father.

"We'll take care of infiltrating the castle, Alborn!" she declared boldly.

Elyon stifled a laugh as Irma clapped her hands to her face in frustration. "Why couldn't Will have kept her big mouth shut?" she squeaked.

What Irma doesn't know, Elyon thought, is that *I'm* going to help.

Stepping forward, Elyon said to Alborn, "I'll go with them. I know the inside of the palace well, so we can easily find our way around."

"Elyon," Alborn said. His red eyes went crinkly around the edges with concern. That was his worried-dad face. Despite the situation, Elyon grinned. She had seen that expression a hundred times. "Are you really sure about this?"

"It's what I want more than anything else, Dad," Elyon said with a smile of confidence. She was almost surprised to realise that that was true.

Maybe being a queen is finally having an

effect, she thought happily.

Whatever the explanation, she now felt eager to get the show on the road. And she wasn't the only one.

Thooom! Thooom! Thooom!

The ceiling high above the rebels' heads pounded again.

"The Annihilators are almost here," Vathek observed, glancing up toward the source of the sound. "Those big, ugly turtles."

"Well, they're one more good reason to get going!" Will said.

The group turned toward the exit hatch of their underground hiding space.

"Not so fast." Vathek looked around at the group, his eyes clouded with concern. He put his hand on Irma's shoulder. "What you're about to do is very dangerous. But I know what you're capable of. Take good care of Elyon."

Elyon blushed. It still surprised her that *she* was at the heart of this conflict. The knowledge made her feel heavy – as if she were a burden for her friends to bear and a problem for them to fix.

Irma, on the other hand, sounded carefree. "You just take care yourself, you big ape," she said. "When I come back, carried triumphantly on the shoulders of the grateful people of Meridian, I want to see your ugly mug in front, cheering for us. Got it?"

"Right," Cornelia said with a smile. "And just to be sure . . ."

Cornelia opened her hands. The white flower she'd been holding – which was Caleb – sat lightly in the middle of her palms, glowing with vitality.

Or perhaps, Elyon thought, swallowing hard, it's glowing with love – with true love, lost forever.

"I'm entrusting you with this," Cornelia murmured as she gently placed the bloom into Vathek's big hands. "You can give it back to me when this whole drama is over."

"It's in excellent hands, Cornelia," Vathek rumbled. Then he looked at all of the girls: Will, whose face was dark with determination; Hay Lin, cheerfully ready for the fight; Cornelia, her drawn face expressing both grief and gumption; and Irma and Taranee, each trying not to look too terrified.

Finally, Vathek gazed down at Elyon. She was the Light of Meridian, the sister of the rebels' most bitter foe, and the very hub of the war to come.

"The crown awaits you," Vathek said simply. "Good luck, girls."

Such a casual send-off, Elyon thought. We might be getting ready to take a math test or try out for the football team.

Instead, she thought, gritting her teeth, we're heading off to fight the battle of a lifetime!

TWO

Krrrzzzaaaakkk!

Cedric cringed at the sound of a magic bolt hitting metal. It was all he could do not to clap his hands over his ears. But that he would not do. He couldn't show his master that he doubted his actions.

Phobos, Cedric reflected, was already upset enough. The seemingly impossible had happened: he'd been outwitted by Elyon and her meddling friends. They'd deceived him and completely thwarted him in his attempted takeover of Elyon's powers!

The aftermath of the Guardians' deception had been even worse. The citizens of Meridian – those unkempt, unwashed peasants – had actually risen up against their ruler! Cedric had been shocked by their impudence.

Phobos, though, seemed more concerned at this point with the Crown of Light.

Grabbing the crown in one hand and Cedric's flowing hair in the other, Phobos had left the battle early, leaving his Annihilators to do the grunt work of destroying the Metamoorians. Then he'd returned to the centre of his palace. There he had retreated to a room deep beneath the palace's catacombs. Filled with darkness, the room was, quite simply, a haven for evil. It was there that Phobos conjured up his darkest ideas and designed his black-hearted schemes.

It was there that he had created the Annihilators.

And it was there, at that moment, that he was trying to destroy the Crown of Light.

Fzzzaaaakkk! Kzzzaaaakkk!

"Raaaaarrrrrgggghh!"

Phobos's screams of rage were bestial and terrifying. They shook the walls, cracked the stone floors, and made Cedric's ears ring painfully. Cedric was grateful that the voluminous blue robes he wore hid his trembling.

Not that Phobos would have noticed. He

had eyes only for the crown. Since arriving in the shadowy room, he'd assaulted the platinum headpiece with every form of magic possible. Nothing had had any effect. In fact, the crown looked more beautiful than ever! It lay on the floor in the centre of the room, glowing tauntingly.

The prince glared at it, his eyes practically spitting fire.

He's going to try again! Cedric thought breathlessly.

Sure enough, Phobos thrust out his hands. Twin blasts of smoking blue magic shot from his palms, hitting the headpiece with another tooth-grinding *FZZAAAKKK!* With the magic still flowing between his hands and the crown, Phobos lifted his arms. The crown floated into the air, shuddering and shimmying in the grip of the electric-blue beams of magic.

"Rrrrggggghhh!" Phobos grunted. His arms were shaking with the effort to destroy the shiny metal. Finally, he could take no more. The effort was too much. He dropped his arms and sank to his knees in exhaustion.

Released from Phobos's grip, the crown plummeted to the marble floor, bouncing on the tiles and making little clinking sounds. It rolled to a halt a few feet away from the shuddering prince.

To Cedric, it appeared as though Phobos's magic had not only not harmed the crown but had in fact strengthened it! The large stone – an oval of brilliant amethyst that sat in the middle of the headpiece – seemed to be glowing brighter than before, pulsing with an indestructible power.

"Nothing!" Phobos muttered, scooping the crown up and staring at it in befuddlement. "Blast! *Nothing* is happening."

Suddenly, Phobos turned around to look at Cedric. The servant ducked his head, trying not to look directly into his master's furious, fiery eyes.

"Look at it, Cedric," he growled.

Cedric slowly raised his head to look at his master.

Phobos shook the headpiece feebly. "I've tried to destroy this in every way imaginable, but it doesn't bear a single scratch. Why?"

Phobos banged the crown onto the floor again and again.

"Why? Whyyyyyyy? WHYYYYYYYY?"

Overcome with fury, Phobos flung the crown into the air, where it moved like a spinning top. The headpiece flew so fast it almost whistled, hitting the wall of the room with a tremendous *bang*, then bouncing back into the air and heading straight for Phobos.

Cedric tried to speak, taking a faltering step toward the prince. But there was no time to intervene. The crown zinged toward Phobos's face like a missile. It came so close that one of its pointed spikes sliced into Phobos's cheek, leaving an angry red wound just below his right eye.

"Aaagh!" he gasped, more surprised than hurt.

Cedric was absolutely terrified. His invincible lord had been struck! What could that mean?

And what should he do?

"Please stop, sire," Cedric gasped, approaching the prince with tentative steps. "Taking it out on that crown won't do any good."

"No!" Phobos said, flinging his arm out to stop Cedric in his tracks. "Giving up is for weaklings."

With that, Phobos's eyes narrowed. He turned to his servant, hissing like a snake. "Do *you* believe I am defeated, Cedric?"

"Oh, no!" Cedric shrilled. "I wasn't saying that, Your Luminousness."

"But, I am," Phobos spat. "All about me are signs of defeat. Look around you, and for once, try not to see things through the eyes of a lowly servant."

Cedric, of course, obeyed. He glanced around the room. It was unfurnished except for a flower-shaped cistern in the centre of it. All the power Phobos had stolen from Meridian's atmosphere converged within it. From that source, Phobos drew his power.

The vessel usually overflowed with glittering magic. Now, however, only the dimmest remnants of Metamoor's energy were left.

"This world is dying!" Phobos roared. "I consumed it, and now everything is in ruins."

The prince pointed a shaky finger at the Crown of Light, which lay in the corner, winking and pulsating.

Cedric stumbled over and gingerly picked the crown up.

"Absorbing my sister's powers should have

been the simplest victory," Phobos said bitterly. "And the greatest. Yet, just as I am unable to bend that ring of metal, I have also been unable to bend Elyon's will. The fault lies with the spell cast upon that crown."

Instinctively, Cedric moved the metal further into the folds of his robe. He was anxious to remove the vexing symbol from his master's sight.

"The fault is mine, Cedric," Phobos continued. He walked to the centre of the room and knelt at the now-empty basin. "I drew my power from the energy of Metamoor, but I've used it all up. And you realise what that means, don't you?"

Cedric's mouth went dry. He was not used to hearing defeat in his master's voice. "Don't say such things, Your Highness," he croaked.

Phobos shrugged off his words. "If I am destined to fall, I will do so holding my head high," he declared. "If I can't have this city – then it will belong to no one!"

Phobos's face suddenly brightened. He squinted. Cedric could see that the wheels of his master's mind were turning, and he caught his breath hopefully. When Phobos schemed, great evil happened. It almost warmed Cedric's reptilian heart.

As usual, his master did not disappoint.

"I will take her on for the last time," he declared.

He began to stalk out of the room. Over his shoulder he added, "The victor's prize will be that very crown. A crown that I now place in your care."

Cedric gulped. He pulled the headpiece from his robe and held it out in front of him. "Prince, I – "

"I know. You're afraid you won't be able to protect it," Phobos said, stopping in the doorway to glance back at Cedric. Now that he'd made his decision, his face had softened. Even the angry gash in his cheek seem to have dwindled to a thin, benign scratch. Phobos was back in control.

Perhaps, Cedric thought reverentially, my prince is already hatching a way to win his battle with Elyon. He will find a way to cheat her of all her power! And then I, in turn, will be the servant of all servants. I will achieve my dream – serving evil forever!

But, he thought then, if I fail to keep this crown safe, how can the plan possibly succeed? With the crown, Elyon's powers will be limitless.

"I am going to turn you into the perfect caretaker," Phobos said, addressing Cedric's silent worry. "I still have enough power to play this game to the very end."

"And I will follow you all the way," Cedric said with a grateful gasp. "What is your command?"

"One more small sacrifice," Phobos said, drawing the phrase out lazily.

Sacrifice? Cedric thought apprehensively.

"If all goes as I believe it will," Phobos said, "you will be handsomely rewarded, Cedric. At long last, you will be admitted into my court of Murmurers."

Again, Cedric gasped. This was the dream he'd worked for all his life! Cedric crouched near his master's feet. "I am at your service, Your Highness," he whispered.

Without pausing for even an instant, Phobos flung a beam of magic at his servant.

"Ughhhh!" Cedric grunted. The magic hit his chest like a sledgehammer, forcing the air painfully from his lungs.

Kzaaaapppp!

Now another blast pummeled Cedric's head, squeezing his skull until he was sure it would shatter. At the same time, he felt his guts roiling, heaving, and heating up.

Cedric had never known such pain. Through the hum of his own agony, through the screams emanating involuntarily from his own throat, he could just barely hear the prince's declaration.

"Rejoice, Cedric!" Phobos cackled. "This is your first step toward a new existence."

"Aaaaaghhhhh!" Cedric screamed.

He collapsed. His hands, scrabbling at the cold floor, were no longer human. Nor were they the green, clawed, scaly hands of his serpentine self.

Instead, they seemed to belong to something monstrous and utterly grotesque.

"Prepare to be reborn!" Phobos bellowed.

Kzaaaaapppp!

He hit Cedric with a final blast of magic.

"Aiiigggggghhhhheeeee!"

Cedric's cries were no longer identifiable. They belonged to no man and no animal. He felt the remnants of his already blackened soul drain from his mind as his body completed its transformation. He had become something unearthly, something truly horrific.

Just before his wretched self folded irrevocably into his new identity, he heard his master's final decree.

"You will be stronger and crueler!" the prince screamed. "For Phobos orders it so!"

THREE

Frost the Hunter sniffed the air. Immediately, his senses were assailed by the odors of daily life in Meridian.

None of those odors, however, were the scents Frost was looking for. He shook his head in annoyance.

You're a hunter, he snarled at himself. The greatest hunter in all of Metamoor! Finding the girl should be an easy task.

Flaring his bright blue nostrils, Frost inhaled once more.

There! There it was: the scent he'd been looking for. A wisp of Princess Elyon's perfume and a hint of soap.

It all matched the scrap of fabric Cedric had given him.

I'm on the trail, Frost thought with satisfaction. He breathed deeply, savoring the scent of his prey with hunger and a small amount of relief.

For Frost was not accustomed to failure.

The blue hunter had been in Prince Phobos's service for years. Never once had he lost his prey. But Frost's winning streak had ended the moment Princess Elyon and the Guardians of the Veil had showed up in Meridian.

The girls spoke in weird tongues. They giggled and grinned and swooned over boys – even Metamoorian boys, like the rebel Caleb.

They seemed more fragile than silk.

Yet they'd beaten Frost, not once but twice. Every time they'd invaded Meridian, Frost had given chase. And every time, the girls had slipped through his claws.

But not this time, Frost vowed as he turned a corner onto an especially dark Meridian street. This time, I *will* not be beaten. I will be redeemed – and rewarded – by Prince Phobos.

"The time has come!" Frost announced to the crew of henchmen he was leading. They had been following behind silently while Frost stalked ahead. The crew was made up of five portly thugs with flame-coloured scales and collars of sharp, white spikes. A few of them grinned at Frost eagerly. The others shifted restlessly from one stumpy leg to the other.

Frost held up a calloused blue hand to still them. "I hear something," he rasped, after a pause.

"I truly hope so," said the lead henchman, whose name Frost had never bothered to learn.

The orange creature fiddled with a gold medal hanging from his plump neck as he continued. "We've gone through every neighbourhood," he said, "and found nothing!"

Frost's lip curled in annoyance at the naysayer, then sniffed the air once more. He cocked his head and listened hard. Finally, he moved farther down the cobblestoned road and knelt before a large, metal disk embedded in the street. The edges were sealed, preventing anyone from easily getting in. But that was just a small inconvenience.

"Yes!" Frost breathed, not bothering to hide his eagerness as he came closer to his prey. He pointed at the disk. "The gown's trail leads right down here."

"Open that drain cover!" cried the creature wearing the medal.

It took the soldiers only seconds to pry the heavy hatch open. Frost jumped through it, landing with a thud on the floor beneath. Ignoring the pain in his feet, he hurried down a corridor. He paused once to sniff the air, and then continued on. After turning only one corner, his thin lips tightened into a rare smile.

"I wasn't mistaken," he boasted to his soldiers, who had followed him. He pointed at some faint smudges on the floor. The group approached and looked at the marks in bewilderment. "Look at these *footprints*," he said in explanation. "This is the rebels' hideaway."

Frost fell to all fours and took a deep whiff of one of the smaller footprints, trying to get an idea of when the prints had been made.

"The trail is fresh," he muttered. "They can't have left this place long ago, and the princess is among them."

"Get going, men!" the lead soldier blurted to the others. "Hurry!"

"Yesssss," Frost said excitedly. "The gown. The gown is nearby!"

"Keep your eyes open!" cried the soldier

wearing the medal. "If Elyon is anywhere near here, she won't be alone. Be ready to – huh?"

Frost had been drifting down the corridor with his eyes closed, his nose guiding him. He'd also been listening for the sound of Elyon's breath, shallow and fearful in some nearby hiding place. Now he opened his eyes and looked around.

At the sound of a soldier's gasp, Frost looked up. "What?" he bellowed. He ran ahead to see what the soldiers were staring at. Something lay in a heap on the floor – something that was filled with the princess's scent. But it was definitely *not* the princess.

"It's . . . her gown!" Frost said, staring incredulously at the discarded pile of silk and lace on the floor.

"I can see that with my own two eyes," a soldier blustered. "But where's the princess? Where are the rebels?"

Frost shook his head. He couldn't speak, couldn't reason. His mind was humming with so much rage that he almost failed to hear the exclamation of one of his henchmen.

"The rebels are up there!" the creature cried.

Frost glanced up. He was surprised to see the fleshy blue face of Vathek grinning at him from a curved catwalk. The walkway was soldered to the side of a giant, metal tank.

Frost scowled in disappointment at the mountainous blue man. Just the mere sight of Frost made Vathek burn with rage. They had once fought on the same side. It had been a strong team – until Vathek had defected to the side of the rebels. Now Vathek was a friend to the Guardians. He was actually protecting the princess from Phobos.

"Heads up, guys!" he called, waving his pudgy hands exuberantly. "Here we are!"

"It's that traitor, Vathek," one of the soldiers hissed.

"We were waiting for you," Vathek said, leaning casually on the catwalk's metal guardrail. "Unfortunately, the princess had a prior engagement. Feel free to wait, if you wish. But if I were you . . ."

Vathek turned slyly to a large dial jutting out from the tank.

". . . I'd look for a nice dry place to run to!"

Frost gaped as Vathek gave the wheel a

hearty spin, then ran to a doorway and whispered to an unseen helper. Vathek had forgotten – or didn't care – that Frost's sharp ears would pick up every word he uttered.

"We're ready!" Vathek cried to his fellow rebel. "Flood the tunnel."

Ffffsssssssshhh!

It didn't take supernaturally strong ears to pick up the next sound – a tremendous gush of water!

"Aaaagggh!" screamed one of Frost's henchmen.

"Let's get out of here!" another shrieked.

"Out, out!" Frost ordered his crew. "Everyone, retreat!"

Dashing ahead of the soldiers, Frost began to run away from the fast-approaching flood. He had to find a way to outrun the water. What did he care if those dopes drowned? They were replaceable – unlike Princess Elyon, whom Frost had lost yet again!

Whoooosh! Fsssssssh! Whoooosh!

A plume of water crashed out of a corridor into the group's path; that geyser was met by a gushing stream from another corridor; a third rush of water soon joined the flow; and all of the streams converged upon the crew, sweeping them off their feet.

"No-o-o-o!" Frost heard one of his men yell from somewhere behind him. "They've opened all the drainage pipes!"

"It's a trap!" Frost growled. "We're getting out of here."

"It's too late!" the soldier shrieked.

Frost would have contradicted him – if the statement hadn't been true! Another huge swell of dirty, cold water swept over Frost's hunters. This time it filled the entire area, turning the walkway into a rushing river The situation seemed hopeless.

"Raaarrrrgggggh!" Frost roared, before his head was submerged in the blue foam.

But Frost wasn't scared: he was too angry to be scared. He fought to live only so that he could complete his quest. His head found the surface of the water.

"Wrrrrraahhhh!" he roared as he flailed on the surface of the torrent. As he tumbled along, occasionally bumping into one of his own men, he glanced up. Vathek and his red-and-green-skinned companion had scurried to a higher catwalk. Frost recognised the companion as

another traitor – Commander Alb
creatures gazed down at Frost with
amusement and disbelief.

"I didn't think they'd fall into our trap,"
Vathek admitted to Alborn quietly – but not so
quietly that Frost's angry ears couldn't pick up
what he'd said.

"I wasn't even sure they'd find their way
down here," the commander replied, looking at
Vathek with excitement. "It was a gamble, yet
we won! Frost and his gang are going to be
swimming around the canals of Meridian for
some time! Who knows? A little dip might just
bring them to their senses."

Frost sneered up at the two traitors before
the water carried him out of sight and into
another tunnel – a tunnel that ended at an
opening in the side of a cliff! Along with the rest
of his crew, Frost was spewed into the air, then
sent hurtling face first into the murky river
where all of Meridian's rainwater – and filth –
came to rest.

Frost roared once more as he hit the water.
It wasn't a roar of triumph or gratitude, though.
Instead, it was full of frustration – and embar-
rassment.

One of his henchmen hit a sandbank and hauled himself out of the water. "They've made laughingstocks of us," the man groaned.

"I know, blast it," Frost replied, brushing a clump of wet hair out of his eyes. "The rebels and the people of Meridian are still free. And what's worse – I didn't manage to find Elyon!"

FOUR

Wow, Irma thought as she looked around. So far, this mission isn't too bad.

After a sneaky trip through the streets of Meridian, the Guardians and Elyon had finally arrived in the garden that surrounded Phobos's palace. As Irma took in the elaborate structure of the palace and the gorgeous grounds, she whistled under her breath.

As a matter of fact, she thought, this mission is downright beautiful!

She was especially captivated by the thorny thicket of black roses at the girls' left. The flowers had petals of a deep, dark black.

I know those roses are poisonous, she thought. But I can't help loving them. They're absolutely the most gorgeous flowers I've ever seen. And they're in Meridian. Go figure!

The prince's palace loomed in the distance. Outfitted with turrets, ramparts, and dramatically arched Gothic windows, it was literally Irma's dream palace – it looked as if it had sprung from the pages of a book of fairy tales.

Irma looked over at Elyon, amazed that this was her friend's home.

At the moment, Elyon wasn't nearly as taken with the palace as Irma was. She was gazing up at the dark windows, looking pale and shaky.

"I – I don't know if I can do it," she whispered.

All the Guardians gathered around her.

"Of course you can do it," Will insisted, patting Elyon's shoulder. "We'll be right there beside you."

Elyon nodded absentmindedly. "Looking at it from here," she said, turning her back on the palace, "that place scares me. I – I don't know if I'll be able to stand up to Phobos!"

"Oh, come on," Irma snorted. "All you have to do is go in, get the crown back, and come out again."

Irma made her voice as light as possible. She didn't want to betray her real fear: that prying the Crown of Light from Phobos's grip was about as doable as getting an A plus on her French final.

Turning things into jokes was, in a way, Irma's job – one of her distinct roles in the world of W.I.T.C.H. – just as it was Hay Lin's gig to sketch a solution to every challenge the girls ran into, Will's to be the group's leader, and Taranee's to be the quiet voice of reason.

And then there's Cornelia, Irma thought, with a sly grin. Where does she stand in our group vibe? *I'd* say that our earth girl stands in the mud, like a stick. A stick-in-the-mud!

Irma was just about to share this brilliant witticism with her friends when Taranee went into active mode.

"We're all set to go," Taranee told Elyon, giving her shoulder a reassuring squeeze. "We can totally take the prince by surprise."

"Yeah!" Hay Lin chirped up. "I bet he still hasn't gotten over the shock he had at the coronation."

"I know," Will added enthusiastically. "The trick of using Elyon's astral drop really worked."

"It was a great idea," Elyon said. "He crowned my double, thinking it was me. So the double died instead of the real me!"

"And from the face he made once he put the crown on," Irma quipped, "I don't think he liked our little trick very much."

"He'll *never* forgive you," Elyon giggled; her friends' words were cheering her up. "You ruined his horrible plan."

"That?" Irma laughed. "Horrible? *You* should have seen the play Hay Lin put on for Christmas. It was so awful that at the end, the audience didn't throw normal eggs. They threw ostrich eggs!"

"Hee-hee-hee!" Hay Lin giggled, laughing along with Irma. Of course, as one of Irma's best friends, Hay Lin knew that Irma had actually *loved* her play and was just joking.

Thinking about the topic of the play, Irma smiled.

It was a myth about us Guardians, she thought. Except that, in the play, we were represented by flying dragons and a magical nymph, all of whom ended up forming Asia's main rivers and mountain ranges. Now *that's* what I call power.

"Oooh!"

"Huh?" Irma said. She'd been pulled out of her feel-good moment by a growl of frustration from Cornelia. The blonde girl was standing nearby, gritting her teeth, clenching her fists, and *glowering* at her friends.

Uh-oh, Irma thought. Talk about power! Dragons and vengeful nymphs have got nothin' on Cornelia's rage.

As if to demonstrate that very point, Cornelia yelled, "That's enough!"

"Eeep!" Hay Lin squeaked, swallowing her giggles with a guilty glance over at Irma.

"This is no time for kidding around, Irma," Cornelia blustered. "We still have a score to settle with Phobos."

"Hey!" Irma protested. "I was just trying to lighten things up a bit."

"Lighten things up?" Cornelia fumed. She stomped over to Irma. "Why can't you just be serious for once in your life?"

"Now, you listen to me, big mouth," Irma retorted. "I – "

"Hold it, guys!" an authoritative voice said.

Will had just stepped between Irma and Cornelia, looking very much the leader. She turned to Cornelia, whose face suddenly went cloudy. Cornelia's anger seemed to melt away, replaced by a shadow of grief.

In spite of herself, Irma felt a pang of sympathy. She'd almost forgotten that Cornelia had just suffered one of the biggest tragedies of her life – she'd seen her true love, Caleb, transformed into a flower just when she and he had finally found each other.

"Cornelia," Will said softly. Cornelia hunched her shoulders and turned away from Will, but Will pressed on. "Irma was just trying to encourage us. You know she wasn't trying to upset anyone."

"Please, Will!" Cornelia whispered, trying to stay strong. "There's no need to be the teacher or anything. Don't treat me like a child. We're here to defeat Phobos. . . ."

Saying that out loud seemed to jolt Cornelia out of her self-pity party. She lifted her gaze from the grass, and a bit of colour returned to her angular cheeks.

"So let's go and do it!" she continued. "I don't want to wait one more second!"

"Okay!" Will agreed with a grin. She turned to peer deeper into the garden through an arch adorned with colourful flowers.

"Daltar?" she called.

A few seconds later an emerald-green face peeked through the flowery archway. Irma sighed with relief.

I'm always happy when we encounter a face here that's familiar *and* friendly, she thought. Not that it happens very often! But Daltar is definitely a good guy.

He also has a sad story – one of thousands in this bleak world, Irma thought.

Daltar was Phobos's gardener. Years earlier, when the prince ordered him to create a thicket of poisonous black roses, the gardener had refused.

So what did Phobos do? Irma thought indignantly. He went ahead and turned Daltar's wife and daughter into the first of the black blooms! After that, anybody who touched the roses' thorns turned into black flowers themselves, and before long, Daltar had an entire grove to care for, never knowing which flowers were his loved ones. And now, he's stuck here, desperately keeping these flowers alive, praying for the day when the curse is broken.

And he's helping us, Irma thought.

The first time Daltar had met Will, she had just been pricked by a black rose. Daltar had saved her, and ever since, he'd been the Guardians' loyal friend.

He was smiling at the girls as he ducked through the arch. "Here you are!" he said enthusiastically. "I've been expecting you! I was worried you'd never show up. The prince came back and he was furious. News of a revolt has come from the city. What's really going on?"

"We'll tell you about it when we have the time," Will said. "But now you have to leave the castle for good. Pretty soon, this place won't be safe at all."

Daltar's green face grew pale. He turned to the rose thicket, his red eyes scanning the blooms.

"Leave?" he rasped. "Never. I can't abandon my garden and these roses – "

Daltar swallowed the end of his sentence as tears sprang to his eyes. Irma suddenly felt a little choked up herself.

It looked as though she wasn't the only one moved by Daltar's devotion.

"The Guardians told me all about this place, Daltar," Elyon said. She stepped out of the cluster of Guardians and approached the gardener, who was staring sadly at the ground.

"Each one of these enchanted roses," Elyon went on, "holds a person within it."

"Oh, Princess," Daltar sighed in acknowledgment.

Elyon placed a hand on one of Daltar's shoulders.

Straightening, Daltar looked into the princess's eyes. Irma could tell he was surprised to see much of his own pain mirrored in Elyon's blue eyes.

"The cruelty committed by my brother," Elyon said, "makes me suffer more with each passing moment. But I promise you that – "

Fwoooommm!

Wow, Irma thought. Talk about a way to kill the mood.

The mood killer she was referring to was a fireball that had just rocketed into the garden. It had come dangerously close to Elyon's head!

"Look out!" Will shouted as Daltar and Elyon both leaped backward, gasping.

The Guardians spun around to face their invaders. Stomping through the arch were two of Phobos's mutant soldiers.

"The Annihilators!" Will cried.

Ugh, Irma thought, looking with disgust at the robotlike fighters. Those guys look like something out of a scary movie. They're red-eyed Godzillas, complete with magic, laser-shooting eyes and all the grace of a couple of rhinoceroses.

The Annihilators' footsteps shook the ground. With their giant fists curled at their sides, they glared at the girls with emotionless evil.

"Well," Irma began. "Seven against two. It won't be a fair fight, but who cares?"

Feeling confident, Irma lifted her hands and began to summon up her magic. As her finger-tips sparked with bright blue energy, she felt power zing up her arms. It made her feel light and breathless.

I think I'll give these guys a nice, cold rinse, thought Irma.

She was just about to shoot her first blast of watery magic, when Cornelia's voice stopped her.

"Save your strength, Irma!" Cornelia called from somewhere behind the water girl.

With her fingers still tingling with power, Irma glanced over her shoulder.

Whoa!

Cornelia's fingers were doing a lot more than tingling. They were shooting off green lightning bolts! The brilliant bursts spun around one another like snakes. They whirled and danced until they merged into one giant ball of earthly energy.

Cornelia held the magical orb before her and turned to face the Annihilators.

The soldiers were oblivious, of course. They continued to stomp toward her, preparing to zap their willowy blonde foe with lasers.

That just shows how little these dudes know about us, Irma thought with satisfaction. When Cornelia gets mad, *nobody* had better mess with her!

"Earth!" Cornelia suddenly roared, "Swallow them up! Remove all evil from this garden!"

She lobbed her magical orb at the baddies' chunky feet.

Kra-KOOOOOMMMM!

The ground on which the Annihilators stood cracked open like an eggshell. What began as a small fissure widened until it was a pit. Rumbling, the pit became a gorge – a gorge that swallowed two of the Annihilators whole. The villains' mouths formed little *o*'s of surprise as they plummeted into the abyss. The Guardians, Elyon, and Daltar crowded at the pit's edge to watch.

After Irma waved goodbye to the baddies, she turned to Hay Lin. "Cornelia scares me when she gets angry," Irma whispered.

"Then, from now on," Hay Lin quipped back, "try not to make her lose her patience."

Irma nodded before peering back into Cornelia's canyon. By now, the Annihilators had disappeared into its depths.

Well, at least one battle's over with, Irma thought. However, the Annihilators are nothing compared to Phobos.

Apprehensively, Irma glanced up. The palace seemed to loom over the Guardians with even more menace than before.

Phobos is probably watching this whole little show, Irma suddenly realised with a shiver. Maybe he even knew that his Annihilators would be no match for us. He didn't care, because he knows what the *real* main event is going to be. The battle of the century – between Elyon and Phobos!

FIVE

The Oracle of Candracar was a solitary man. Every day, he spent most of his time meditating in his temple in the clouds.

While his closest adviser, the white-bearded Tibor, stood behind his right shoulder, the Oracle would watch over several worlds. He would tap into the citizens' feelings – their joy and their pain. He would conjure up images in the vapors of his sacred lily pond. Or he would summon a magical orb with a flick of his magic fingertip. Through that orb he'd observe the inhabitants of the earth, Metamoor, and countless other worlds. He would sense the state of the Veil. And he would listen to the desires of people throughout the universe.

Five people, in particular, really piqued his interest.

The Guardians of the Veil had been much on the Oracle's mind of late.

The Oracle floated through a long, golden corridor and came to a halt in one of Candracar's most hallowed spaces – the meeting hall of the Congregation. The round auditorium was sun-splashed and airy. Iridescent clouds shimmered just outside its windows, filling the hall with a sweet scent and a steady, gentle mist.

In the centre of the floor of the splendid hall was a round mosaic made of stones bluer than a Caribbean lagoon, shells more iridescent than the rarest opals, and swaths of crystal, emerald, and sapphire.

When the Oracle arrived in the hall, the Congregation had already assembled on the tiered benches. The Oracle perched himself upon a small podium floating in the centre of the room. Tibor rustled into place behind him.

The Oracle's sea- coloured eyes were steady as he scanned the Congregation. His benign smile did not waver. He was concerned about the state of the Guardians and the Veil, but beneath that concern was absolute faith – a much stronger sentiment.

The same, perhaps, cannot be said of my fellow elders, the Oracle thought with a small sigh. I can sense deep agitation in the congregants, from the contentious Luba to the sleepy-looking Bolgo. They are nervous, perhaps even afraid.

This meeting, the Oracle predicted to himself, will be full of disagreement. We are all so different, yet we have the same goal: to save the universe from Prince Phobos's destructive wrath. To preserve good. To abolish evil.

Even, the Oracle thought with a grimace, if some of our methods are unorthodox.

The Oracle signaled to the congregants in the room to be silent. All restless movement ceased. Luba, Bolgo, and the other creatures grew quiet, bowing their heads reverentially.

"I've said it before, and I'll say it again," the Oracle began. "Something I had not foreseen is happening."

As the Oracle explained to the Congregation the details of the rebellion in Meridian, his voice soared through the hall.

"At times, that which centuries cannot

displace," the Oracle observed, "is destroyed in an instant. The Guardians are battling for the liberation of Meridian."

"With what consequences, Oracle?" Bolgo piped up. His bright-pink skin flushed a shade rosier as he added, "Perhaps we should intervene! Those girls – "

"No, Bolgo," the Oracle insisted gently. "Those girls have done much more than was asked of them in working for the good of Meridian."

The Oracle lifted his hands, bringing his upturned palms together to create a miniature stage. With one nod of his graceful head, an image suddenly appeared above the small platform. The scene was chaotic. Tiny Metamoorian creatures were waving wooden clubs and running toward a phalanx of soldiers. The citizens looked tired, and their eyes were filled with a combination of rage and terror. They were no match for the well-armed soldiers.

Yet the underdogs pressed on.

"Within their hearts," the Oracle proclaimed, "lives pride."

The scene floating above the Oracle's

cupped hands took on texture and nuance. The grey streets of Meridian came into focus, so that the soldiers and rebels no longer battled in thin air. The Congregation watched as Vathek, a good-souled creature who'd defected from Phobos's side, led the rebels bravely, directing them toward a cluster of soldiers.

"They have courage," the Oracle sang out.

Pitchforks blocked swords. Clubs deflected axe blades.

"Freedom!" the Oracle announced as his hologram shifted once again. Now the Metamoorians had trapped the soldiers! Blocking the orange-skinned thugs' escape route, the rebels were ordering the soldiers to place their weapons in the dirt.

The Oracle crossed his arms, slipping his hands into the bell-shaped cuffs of his sleeves. Instantly, his visual aid disappeared, leaving behind a wisp of fog.

"By attacking his sister publicly," the Oracle explained, "Phobos believed he could impose his will upon his subjects once again. But he committed the gravest of errors."

The Oracle closed his eyes. With the facts outlined for the congregants, it was now time to make a decision, a plan of action. The Oracle searched his soul for wisdom.

The answer came to him almost instantly.

"The Congregation," he decreed, "will not intervene. We will wait and calmly observe what happens."

With grace, the Oracle rose. Nodding respectfully to the Congregation, he began to float out of the hall.

That did not mean, however, that he left his followers' midst. Oh, no. The Oracle saw all, and he certainly *heard* all. Even as he glided into the corridor, the Oracle heard the congregants' exclamations and felt their emotions.

Bolgo, for instance, was whispering to two of his compatriots. "There's something the Oracle is not telling us," Bolgo murmured anxiously. "While we stand around talking, the Guardians could be in danger. If Phobos captures Elyon, nothing will stop him from taking over her powers. And if *that* happens – "

"We'll begin to worry then."

The Oracle lifted his eyebrows slightly upon hearing the reedy voice – it belonged to the Congregation's newest member, Yan Lin. She was a former Guardian whose strength had stayed with her even when her body grew old and weak.

"We will only worry," Yan Lin continued, her voice growing stronger, "if Phobos does succeed."

"Yan Lin!" one of the members said in a burbly, watery voice. "Now you're talking just like the Oracle."

"No, my old friend," the lady countered. "I speak as a grandmother, one who knows her granddaughter."

The Oracle smiled.

The older woman was talking, of course, about Hay Lin, the Guardian of the air.

Hay Lin was indeed a sprite to be reckoned with, the Oracle agreed silently. He still remembered the day Yan Lin had told the five Guardians about their destinies, anointing each girl with her unique power. As for the Heart of Candracar, Yan Lin had handed it over to Will.

All five girls had been surprised by their new roles.

It's understandable, the Oracle thought. One moment, they were simple schoolgirls. The next, they were put in charge of saving the world. Cornelia fought off her own magic as hard as she could. Taranee recoiled from it in fear. Irma thought it was more a game than a destiny.

And Hay Lin? Well, she might have heaved a shaky breath or two, but it didn't take long for her to embrace her fate.

"I was once a Guardian myself," Yan Lin told the nervous group, "and I say that Hay Lin and her friends are stronger than you think!"

The Oracle nodded in agreement. Then he continued on his journey through the corridor.

Yes, Yan Lin, he thought. The Guardians have strength that is still untapped. And for the final battle that awaits them, they're going to need every bit of it!

SIX

As the Guardians followed behind Elyon into Phobos's palace, they gasped. The luxurious castle was breathtaking!

Cornelia had never been one to be impressed by fine places and things. She'd grown up in a beautiful apartment, with a closet packed with trendy clothes and a bed piled with lacy pillows. Of all her friends, Cornelia had the cushiest life.

All my friends, Cornelia corrected herself, except Elyon! This palace is unbelievable!

Like this foyer, for instance, Cornelia thought as the girls crept through the palace's entrance hall. It has marble pillars, a stone floor etched with the most delicate little flowers, and gold leaves engraved *everywhere*. It's bigger than the biggest ballroom I've ever seen.

Much to Cornelia's annoyance, Irma was whistling as she scurried across the foyer ahead of Elyon.

Never mind that Elyon should be the one leading the way, Cornelia thought drily.

Irma glanced over her shoulder at the princess. "Wow!" she gushed. "Is this really your house?"

"Yes, Irma," Elyon said with a little nod of her head.

Cornelia had a feeling, though, that Elyon's answer was not as lighthearted as it sounded.

All my life, Cornelia thought, Heatherfield has been my home. I've been as sure of that as anything. It's like, my name is Cornelia Hale, I have an irritating little sister named Lilian, I go to school at Sheffield Institute, and I live in Heatherfield.

Elyon, Cornelia was sure, had always felt the same way. Their seaside city, with its rocky beach, its park, and its abundance of cute, dreamy boys, was the only home Elyon had ever known.

Now, she'd been transported to Meridian,

where there were no parks, few friends, and a brother intent on stealing her powers and causing her harm!

Oh, Elyon, Cornelia thought, gazing at her friend with a sigh. Meridian is your destiny, but it's also a place that's caused you a lot of pain. It's both a sanctuary and a curse.

Blinking in surprise, Cornelia realised that the same could be said for Metamoor.

If I'd never come here, she thought, I wouldn't have found Caleb.

You could definitely say, Cornelia thought wryly, that I have a love-hate relationship with this place.

As if she were channeling Cornelia's thoughts, Elyon spoke up again.

"This is where I belong now," she said to Irma quietly, "even though I really miss Heatherfield."

"No problem!" Irma joked. "If you want, we can swap! As soon as I get back, I'll try to convince my folks and – "

"Shhhh!" Will interrupted, holding up her hand. She had come to a halt in front of a grand marble staircase.

Putting a finger to her lips, Will shushed the

other Guardians and Elyon. "Listen," she said.

The girls held their breath and stood quietly where they were.

Even Irma is following orders! Cornelia thought, eyeing her usually restless comrade. I guess this is serious.

After a few seconds, Taranee whispered, "What? I don't hear anything – except for a creepy silence."

"Even so . . ." Will replied, gazing up the stairs with a suspicious squint. "It's like a vibration. It's coming from the hall at the top of those stairs."

"That's the throne hall," Elyon said. "*Phobos's* throne hall."

Cornelia watched as Elyon clenched her jaw and began climbing the stairs.

"Good," Will said, following close behind. Elyon was shorter and slighter than the Guardians, who were all a good head taller at the moment than they were when they were in their earthly forms. But if she was a pixie, she was a tough one. Her skinny back was straight, and her steady pace never wavered.

Cornelia couldn't help feeling proud as she followed her friend up the stairs. Unfortunately, this was not the time for warm, fuzzy thoughts. Will was in battle mode.

"Let's keep our eyes peeled," Will told the crew, "and move quietly."

As the girls neared the top of the staircase, a light emanating from the throne hall grew brighter and brighter. It spilled over the top of the stairs, flooding the Guardians' eyes when they stepped into its splendor. For a moment, it felt as though they had been blinded!

Still, they knew they weren't alone.

A voice had begun echoing off the the high ceiling. The voice was slithery and slimy. The sound made Cornelia's skin crawl, especially when she saw how it taunted her friend.

"*Elyon*," the voice called out. "*Elyon. ELYON!*"

"Here I am, Phobos," Elyon answered.

Cornelia blinked rapidly, eager to dash the spots from her eyes. When her vision finally cleared, she too, saw the evil prince.

Instead of looming over the girls, tall and imperious as usual, he was slumped in a chair, chin resting gloomily on his fists, twists of his hair draped limply around his feet.

Cornelia was surprised. If not for the

silk-upholstered throne he sat on, Phobos would have looked utterly defeated.

He certainly didn't sound defeated, though. He greeted Elyon in a voice dripping with pure sarcasm.

"Here she is, the heir to the throne!" he announced, gesturing to the glittering chair. "This is what you were looking for, isn't it? What are you waiting for? Take it! It's yours."

"I don't want to fight you, Phobos," Elyon said, her voice steady. Cornelia was sure that she was the only one who could hear the slight catch in Elyon's voice.

"I just want all of this madness to stop," Elyon went on, a bit more forcefully now. "And I want you to give up and stand trial."

Phobos got up out of his throne and glided toward the girls. He came to a halt in the centre of the throne hall, standing in the middle of a large mosaic in the floor. Like every other accent in the palace, the mosaic was beautiful.

"Hmmm," Phobos said, rolling his icy eyes. "What a tempting offer. I, however, have something else in mind. What do you say . . . to a duel?"

As Cornelia clenched her fists in rage, Will

stepped forward. "We aren't here to play games with you!" she yelled at Phobos.

Phobos's smooth face went dark. "I wasn't talking to you, little girl," he spat back at the Guardians' leader.

Elyon put a soothing hand on Will's shoulder, then arched an eyebrow at her brother. "What kind of duel did you have in mind?" she asked.

"Elyon!" Cornelia gasped. She couldn't let Elyon do anything foolish. Without thinking, she dashed up behind her friend and whispered in her ear, just as she'd done about a million times back at the Sheffield Institute when she and Elyon had been best friends, passing notes and telling secrets.

"Don't accept," Cornelia warned in a frightened whisper.

Phobos ignored Cornelia and continued his challenge. "A battle of magic powers with no limits," he proposed. "If you win, Meridian will be yours. But if you are defeated, you will put on the Crown of Light, and I will absorb your powers."

"And why should I trust you?" Elyon asked. "You've never been honest with me."

"I simply made an error in calculation, dear sister," Phobos replied with a sinister grin. "If I had gotten rid of you immediately, we wouldn't be here talking now."

Grrrr! Cornelia thought. That guy is the *worst* kind of manipulator. Every word out of his mouth has a double meaning, and every offer is really a threat.

"I have nothing left to lose," Phobos went on, "and this is a challenge you can win, Elyon. My power is growing weaker, while your power is still unfledged and ready to explode. Right now, my sister, we're even!"

Cornelia saw Elyon shift her weight. She was actually considering Phobos's absurd proposal!

"I'm offering you the possibility of rising to the throne," Phobos continued, reaching out a hand enticingly. "You'll be hailed as the saviour of Metamoor."

"Don't listen to him, Elyon!" Will cried.

Elyon barely acknowledged her. Her eyes were locked on Phobos's stare. The siblings seemed to be approaching a standoff!

"Princess Elyon," Phobos said dramatically. "The girl who saved Meridian. The Light of Meridian. The one and only!"

"So be it!" Elyon blurted suddenly. "But I have something else to add to the bargain, brother. When you are defeated, you will pay for everything you've done!"

"Ah," Phobos said with an evil grin. "Proud, with a fighting spirit. That's the Elyon I know."

Aghast, Cornelia made her way over to Will. "We can't just let her fight him!" she whispered into Will's ear.

"You're right," Will replied grimly. "When I give the signal, we'll attack Phobos all together. Ready?"

Cornelia nodded slightly. She glanced at Taranee, Irma, and Hay Lin. They had heard Will, too. Their fingers were already wiggling, summoning up sparks of orange, blue, and silver magic.

Cornelia conjured her own emerald-coloured power. She was ready!

"Now!" Will shouted.

The five girls formed a barricade in front of Elyon. Then, in perfect synchronization, the Guardians charged straight at the malevolent prince.

Upon seeing them advance, the prince simply laughed.

"Poor, foolish girls," he teased cruelly, before casually flinging out his hand.

The blast of white magic that hit Cornelia in the stomach felt like no blow she'd ever experienced. It seemed to swipe at her insides like a magic hook, dragging her backward. She was almost relieved when she finally skidded to a halt on the floor.

Her girlfriends landed next to her, then groaned painfully as they struggled to their feet.

As the Guardians tried to stand, Phobos screamed at them. "This battle has nothing to do with you. It's a family matter, so get lost!"

Yeah, right, Cornelia thought. She planted both palms on the floor and pushed herself up.

That was when something strange happened.

Cornelia's powerful arms didn't catapult her onto her feet as she'd expected. Instead, they sank right into the floor!

Gasping, Cornelia glanced to her right.

Irma's legs were driven thigh-deep into the floor that had now turned a liquidy green colour. Taranee had sunk in up to her rib cage. She was waving her arms at her friends in mute horror.

Will and Hay Lin were powerless to help.

They too, were stuck inside the floor. The jade tiles had melted together to form a sticky mire – some sort of quicksand that was rapidly swallowing the Guardians up.

As Cornelia's chest began to heave in panic, Irma cried out, "What's happening? We're being sucked down into – "

"An old friend is waiting for you with open arms," Phobos interrupted.

Cornelia twisted in the green muck to glare at him.

Phobos stood just beyond their sticky circle, his arms crossed smugly. "You'll see him soon . . . in the Abyss of Shadows!"

Blurp.

Cornelia screamed and turned toward the sound. Taranee had just disappeared below the surface. She was gone!

Blurp. Blurp!

Struggling and shrieking, Hay Lin and Irma disappeared, too.

Will was seconds away from going under as well.

Cornelia calculated that she had about one and a half seconds before the floor claimed her. That was just enough time for her to seek out

Elyon, who was screaming and reaching out for her friends as they quickly sank from her view, one by one.

Elyon's face had gone white.

"Cornelia!" she begged in a shaky voice. "Guys!"

"Elyon!" Cornelia cried. There were so many things she wanted to say to her friend: *Goodbye . I've missed you. I never doubted you* – they were the same things she had never gotten a chance to tell Caleb before he was taken from her forever.

But Phobos had stolen that wish, too, from Cornelia.

Blurp.

Cornelia's head sank beneath the surface. Elyon, and everything else for that matter, disappeared from her view. She began to plummet into pitch darkness! Feeling her long skirt billow up over her head, she scrabbled at the air in terror.

That, of course, was futile. She found no foothold. No trace of light. Nothing.

"Oh, my gosh!" Will cried in fear from someplace just below Cornelia. "Where are we going?"

Surprisingly, someone answered – in a voice that was decidedly *not* welcoming.

Coming from a point high above the girls' heads, the voice was gurgly and craggy. It sounded as though it belonged to a creature made of lava. Cornelia had a very bad feeling about the voice, even before she got the full gist of its answer. "Where are you going?" the speaker repeated. "Straight into the depths of your new nightmare!"

"Ooof!"

Cornelia heard one of her friends grunt as they hit the floor.

Thud. Splat! "Ow!"

That would have been the other three Guardians.

I'm next, Cornelia thought with a cringe.

Crash!

Cornelia groaned as she found herself belly down but miraculously uninjured on a cold, clammy surface. A moment later, she lurched to her feet and felt around for her friends. Finding one another in the blackness, they clustered together.

Hay Lin whispered, "That voice."

"I heard it, too," Taranee piped up. "It sort

of sounded like Cedric's voice, but a lot deeper and a lot more awful!"

"And, what do you know! It *is* me," the voice suddenly boomed, sending echoes bouncing off the cave walls.

So much for keeping secrets, Cornelia thought with a sigh.

"Cedric?" Irma demanded. "Where are you, and *what* happened? With that voice, I'd say you swallowed a porcupine or something."

Suddenly, light flooded the space.

The girls blinked through the glare – then gasped in horror!

Cedric had been transformed into the most disgusting creature Cornelia could ever have imagined.

He had become a giant bug.

His legs were skinny and jointed, like a mammoth grasshopper's. His torso was composed of a series of overlapping shells that resembled the hinged exoskeleton of a cockroach. Hunched into a lumbering slouch, Cedric's long, mega-muscled arms stretched out toward the Guardians with fingers capped by six-inch-long talons.

But the worst part by far was Cedric's face.

That was what made Irma scream, Cornelia blanch, and Taranee stumble backward in shock.

Cedric's gaping mouth was filled with jagged teeth. Atop his head was a strange, conical cap that looked charred and crusty. His eyes bulged, black and soulless.

He was beyond awful – and he was way too happy to see the Guardians.

"Hello again, Guardians," he growled. "What's wrong? Don't you recognise your old friend?"

SEVEN

So, this is what absolute fear feels like, Will thought.

She stood in the enormous, black-walled, cryptlike room that was known as the Abyss of Shadows. She glared up at the horrible red bug that Cedric had become and felt a wave of fear wash over her, making her skin prickly and sweaty.

The thing is, she thought, I never actually wanted to know what absolute fear felt like. I never wanted to save the world, either, much less some world I'd never heard of called Metamoor.

But here I am.

I'm leading the group that's going to restore Elyon to her

throne. *I'm* in charge of the crew that's going to conquer Phobos and Cedric. *I* have to make sure we close the rest of those portals in the Veil. *And* somehow, I have to squeak by in algebra class with a passing grade.

Isn't it funny? Will thought with a tiny whimper. For a moment, I'd started to like being the Keeper of the Heart of Candracar. It felt cool being able to guide my friends or feel them rally behind me when I made a decision.

But when we're facing a monster like this, Will went on, all I want to do is run and hide. It reminds of my first day at Sheffield. I would have given anything that day to get out of Heatherfield and go back to my old home in Fadden Hills.

But eventually, she thought, Heatherfield started to feel like home. And why? Because of my friends! Because of Taranee, Hay Lin, Cornelia, and Irma.

We're a team, Will realised. Which means, when you think about it, that I'm not really on my own at all. With my friends behind me, I feel much stronger.

Glancing at the girls around her and heaving a deep sigh, Will turned her attention back to Cedric. His gravelly voice dripped venom as he hissed at the Guardians.

"You can hide all you want, insolent vermin," he said, "but you'll never escape."

"We'll see about that, Cedric," Will shot back, feeling her confidence build.

"Is that a challenge, little Will?" Cedric growled. "If so, it's a mistake you'll soon regret!"

Will barely saw Cedric's arm moving toward her. It looked like simply a blur of red. Before she could react, Cedric had slammed right into her, hitting her with such a loud *thunkkk* that her ears rang.

She was sent flying.

As she soared through the air, back arched, arms flailing, she unleashed a bloodcurdling scream. Pain sizzled through her muscles like an electric shock.

And Cedric wasn't through with her yet. He began stomping toward her the instant her body hit the floor. His teeth were bared and his talons whistled in the air with each swing of his long, reptilian arms.

"Learn to fear me," the monster bellowed at Will. "Prince Phobos has made me stronger and faster! I'm unstoppable!"

I really can't argue with that, Will thought woozily. She tried to get to her feet, but found that her limbs were now as springy as rubber bands.

I – I can't fight Cedric, she thought frantically. He's going to win.

Not knowing whether to feel angry or resigned, Will braced herself, waiting for another onslaught of Cedric's wrath.

Wzink!

"Raaaaarrrggggh!"

Will cringed again – until suddenly, she realised something.

Hey, she thought in wonder. That roar? It didn't belong to me! In fact, it sounded a lot like ugly old Cedric!

Will's head rolled to the left just in time to see Irma shoot a second jolt of watery magic at Cedric's armored thorax. The gush hit him like a missile, and he screamed again.

Will would have cheered weakly, but suddenly, something pinned her arms to her sides.

Then that same something lifted her clear off the floor! Had one of Cedric's long, claw-tipped limbs grabbed at Will, even as the rest of him was fighting Irma off?

Will glanced up. "Hay Lin!" she managed to yell.

While Irma had distracted Cedric with her magic water bombs, Hay Lin had swept in and plucked Will out of harm's way. As her friend flew Will to a spot in a far corner of the Abyss of Shadows, Will glanced over her shoulder. Irma was continuing her assault on the big bully.

"'Phobos made me stronger and faster,'" she mimicked as she gave his belly another blast. "Every time, the same old line. While he was at it, Phobos could have made you a bit more original."

Cedric growled. He had no witty comeback for the sassiest Guardian.

He did, however, have magic lasers that he could shoot from his eyes!

Will gasped as two orange-red beams now targeted Irma, who yelped and jumped backward. The lethal rays just missed her face, but her wavy, brown hair wasn't completely spared. Oooh, bad hair day, Will thought, as she felt her strength already beginning to return to her. Irma's not going to like that!

Irma, however, just laughed it off. "I don't really care for the trim," she said to Cedric breezily. "Although you did get rid of my split ends! Thanks, dude."

Cedric hissed. "The game is over, girls," he announced darkly.

He reared back.

His eyes began to spark and smoke.

His giant, slimy teeth gnashed menacingly behind a grotesque grimace.

He's in total attack mode, Will thought in a panic. She started to run to her friends' aid.

They, however, were way ahead of her. Standing elbow to elbow, Cornelia, Irma, Hay Lin, and Taranee thrust their arms out together.

"It's over for you, Cedric," Cornelia declared.

The four Guardians slammed the monster with a convergence of blue, silver, green, and orange magic.

Bzap!

Cedric stumbled backward, hitting one of the black walls.

Ftoooommmm!

The chamber rumbled. Unfortunately, as soon as the dust settled, Cedric recovered.

"Hmph," he sneered in his husky voice. "Is

that all you're capable of?"

He flung his arm out to the side, as if he were flicking away an annoying mosquito. Almost accidentally, his claw caught Hay Lin right in the ribs.

Will felt her stomach lurch as she saw Hay Lin – already light as a feather – go flying into another corner of the abyss.

That corner was just as dark and shadowy as the nook where Will was crouched, still recovering from Cedric's blow.

And Hay Lin looked just as woozy now as Will had felt a few minutes earlier. Will saw Hay Lin's fingers flutter to her forehead as her face crumpled up in agony.

"Oh, my head," Hay Lin rasped, just loud enough for Will to hear from her hiding place in the corner.

Will couldn't just sit there. She began began making her way over to Hay Lin's side. She had to help her. Hay Lin continued to moan.

"That big ape really packs a punch," Will heard her murmur. "Ugh . . . hey, what's that?"

Will raised an eyebrow as Hay Lin suddenly seemed to forget her pain and scrambled behind a little wall jutting out from the corner.

Since every surface in the room was as black as tar, Will hadn't noticed the foreshortened wall earlier, or the closet-size nook behind it.

As Hay Lin rummaged in the nook, a burst of light suddenly blazed forth! The light was golden, and as warm and inviting as sunshine. Hay Lin let out a loud gasp.

What's back there? Will wondered. Feeling strength seep into her legs, she moved closer to her friend. She stopped in her tracks, though, when she heard Hay Lin's next exclamation.

"No way!" she breathed. "That's the Crown of Light!"

Peeking over her shoulder, Hay Lin yelled, "Guys! Take a look at what I found. It's Elyon's crown!"

"Don't touch that!" Cedric roared.

Will screamed. The creature's growl had been so guttural, so grating, so completely terrifying that she almost wished he had dealt her another physical blow instead.

Careful what you wish for, Will admonished herself. Clearly, Cedric's life depended upon protecting that crown. There was no way he would give it up without a fight!

EIGHT

Elyon watched the Guardians disappear through the floor one by one. When Taranee went under, Elyon's stomach clenched. Her sadness felt like a hunger pang, only sharper, crueler.

The loss of Hay Lin and then Irma made Elyon clutch at her middle to try to stave off the horrible emptiness.

Will sank beneath the surface of the jade-green tiles, and Elyon's pain grew even stronger.

Finally, Cornelia gave Elyon a sad final wave and disappeared.

Now, Elyon felt as though she were nothing but an empty shell. All her strength seemed to abandon her.

My friends attacked Phobos for *me*, she thought, her mouth dry and parched. And look what happened! They were tricked by Phobos and sent who knows where.

Elyon's grief and outrage were so intense her whole body began to tremble. She stumbled, coming close to cascading into the liquid green circle on the floor herself.

And things were only about to get worse.

Minutes after the Guardians had fallen through the green circle, the throne hall began to shimmy and shake. Sonic booms echoed beneath Elyon's feet, and dust sifted down from the ceiling. Muffled roars filtered up through the floor.

"Huh?" Elyon cried. Because she had no one else to turn to for answers, she reluctantly made eye contact with her brother, who still stood next to his throne, sneering at her.

"What's happening?" Elyon demanded. "That echoing voice shaking the ground is . . ."

"My dear Cedric," Phobos said, gazing fondly down at the floor. "He's taking his well-deserved revenge on your friends."

Elyon's heart began to beat faster.

My friends, she thought. What is Cedric

doing to them? What's more, what is Phobos going to do to me? I guess the Guardians didn't think I could take him on, or they wouldn't have leaped in to try to help me.

She bit her lip, just as Phobos turned his full attention to her.

"Ignore that racket," he ordered Elyon. "*You* and I have a score to settle. Until the bitter end, dear sister."

"Until the bitter end," Elyon repeated softly.

Those ominous words should have filled Elyon's heart with even more terror than she already felt. Instead, they caused something to click in her mind.

This could be it! she thought. My last stand against Phobos. My final shot to save Meridian from my brother's evil – and take my place as the rightful heir to the throne.

If she won that last battle, she realised, her ordeal might finally end. Meridian, the Guardians, Elyon herself – would all be saved.

With that awareness came an eagerness to get on with the duel. She looked up with a defiant gleam in her eye.

"Until the bitter end!" she said again, this time loudly – and with a snarl.

Phobos responded to Elyon's words by hurling a blast of white-hot magic straight at her.

"I never wanted it to come to this, Elyon," he said, gritting his teeth. "You were the one who made things difficult."

Elyon's hands shot up in response. Instinctively, she unleashed a force field from her palms. The magic looked like a translucent, round shield floating in front of her. Phobos's magic crashed into it with a metallic *twannngggg!*

"I opened my eyes," Elyon barked at her brother from behind her magical shield. "I saw what was outside this palace, and I realised that the fault was all yours."

"What you call my fault is what I call ambition," Phobos protested. "This world was brimming with magical power. I merely took what was rightfully mine. With your immense power, I am going to destroy the Veil and cross the threshold of Meridian, ready for new conquests!"

Suddenly, Phobos abandoned his stream of white magic. His hands fell to his sides. He stamped his foot on the marble floor.

Sha-zash!

Elyon dropped her hands, too. Her expression, though, turned to one of shock when she saw what her brother had done. The floor beneath Phobos's feet had begun to undulate like the ocean. Its rubbery waves rippled toward Elyon. When they reached her, they crested, just like whitecaps on the Heatherfield Sea.

Instead of crashing like ocean waves, though, these crests continued their vertical motion. They turned into long, thin tendrils that danced tauntingly around Elyon. Then the tentacles began to snake around Elyon's ankles, slithering up her legs and encircling her hips.

The weird tentacles would have kept going if Elyon hadn't suddenly figured out a way of eluding them!

Thinking about ocean waves made her think of water. And when she thought about water, she also thought about – ice!

Fzap!

Elyon focused all her magical energy on the strangling tentacles. With a quick crackle, they suddenly went silver and white. They were frozen solid! Shooting Phobos a mirthless grin,

Elyon kicked at them with her toe. They shattered into a thousand pieces.

"Sorry to disappoint you, dear brother," she said drily, "but I'm going to make a few changes to your plans."

Phobos shrugged. He flung out his right arm, sending another laserlike blast straight at her.

And just in time, Elyon whipped up another shimmering shield to block it.

"It's useless to try to resist me, Elyon," Phobos called out. "You can't escape your destiny!"

"My destiny was to rise to the throne of Meridian," Elyon retorted. "That was my right, and you defied me."

Phobos closed his hand in a fist. His magic ray evaporated with a *poof*. "Very funny!" he said, cackling. "Since when have older brothers taken orders from little sisters?"

"Since *now*!" Elyon screamed.

She threw her arms into the air, concentrating so hard her brother became nothing more than a blue-and-green blur.

Howling with effort, she unleashed the most destructive, fiery, and deadly blast of magic she'd ever conjured up since she'd arrived in Meridian.

Ba-dooooommm!

An explosion.

Flying bricks.

Smoke and dust.

Elyon hurled herself to the floor and covered her head with her arms, waiting for the destruction she had wrought to settle around her. Even though her jaw was clenched tightly, her teeth, she realised, were chattering loudly.

Cruelty and the desire to wreak devastation on others did not come naturally to her as they did to her brother.

She could only imagine what her adoptive parents and Vathek were thinking at that moment. Surely they'd seen the blast from the city below. Countless other Metamoorians would have witnessed it, too. After all, Phobos had built his ostentatious palace on the city's highest peak, for all to see.

Elyon pictured Vathek's eyes widening. "Alborn," he'd say to her father. "They're battling in the castle."

"I can hear that, my friend," Alborn would reply calmly, as his red eyes clouded over with worry. Then, sighing deeply, he would say, "But there's nothing we can do. Phobos's army has been defeated. That was *our* battle, and we won it."

Miriadel, Elyon's mother, would surely agree with her husband. "We have done what we can. The future of Meridian," she'd say, "now lies in the hands of those girls. And *our* girl. Elyon."

Two tears squeezed out of Elyon's eyes as she imagined her mother's wise words.

Wearily, Elyon hauled herself to her feet. She blinked in awe at the giant hole her magic had ripped in the wall. She shivered slightly as the cool, damp, Metamoorian air rolled into the castle, immediately casting a chill upon the room.

With a sigh, Elyon turned to her brother, expecting to see his fallen form on the floor. He was . . . not dead. He wasn't even down. He stood amid the rubble uninjured, spared by his sister's mercy. She had not had the heart to truly hurt him.

"That blow could have been for you, Phobos," she declared, pointing at the jagged hole in the wall.

Phobos glanced over his shoulder to look at the hole. "How generous of you, Elyon," he sniffed. "Your clemency is touching. Loyalty and compassion. These are genuine signs of true nobility."

Elyon felt her shoulders loosen just a bit. Perhaps Phobos was grateful for his life, after all.

"So, do you give up?" she demanded.

"Ah, Elyon," Phobos said, stepping neatly to the side of a large chunk of plaster that had fallen from the ceiling. "You would be a wonderful princess, if only you hadn't been stupid enough to be enchanted by my words."

Elyon couldn't help being confused. Had she imagined it, or had Phobos just followed a glowing compliment with a scathing insult?

And which was she to believe?

The answer, as usual, came in Phobos's action, not in his words.

He bent and scooped up the heavy chunk of plaster, balancing its weight on his palm. Gazing pensively at it for a moment, he felt its heft in his hand.

Then his lip curled in a sneer.

He looked up at Elyon with fire in his eyes.

And then he hurled the plaster directly at her head!

Tunk!

Elyon grunted as she felt the heavy plaster connect with the back of her skull. She felt pain shoot through her head.

Then she fell.

"*Uhhnn,*" she groaned as she hit the dust-covered floor.

That dust was all she could see. Grey . . . lots of grey . . . grey that was swiftly turning to black.

I'm going to pass out, Elyon thought.

In a panic, she struggled to remain conscious.

How can I fight off Phobos, she thought desperately, lying on the floor like this?

The prince clearly had had the same thought. He was chortling at his victory. As Elyon slipped toward unconsciousness, his voice sounded farther and farther away.

"Our battle ends here, Elyon," he taunted. "And you've lost! As have your meddling friends!"

Sensation was seeping from Elyon's body. Her fingers and toes grew numb. Then her legs lost all feeling. Her very heart seemed to slow. She could hear it thudding ponderously in her ears.

Unfortunately, though, Elyon's emotions were still strong. She was filled with despair, so much so that she was almost relieved when her mind finally slipped into darkness.

NINE

As the Guardians continued to take on the big, buggy version of Cedric, Taranee felt torn.

Should I hit Cedric with a bunch of small fire darts? Or do I go with one big fireball? Do I aim for the eyes or give him a hot foot? When you're trapped in the Abyss of Shadows with a giant, nasty monster, your weapon had better count!

Taking another gander at Cedric's immense size, Taranee decided that the situation definitely called for the giant fireball.

While Cornelia and Irma kept Cedric at bay with an earth-and-water extravaganza – namely, a mud bath – Taranee held out her hands. Immediately, she felt orange magic fizz through her arms. A golf ball–sized sphere of fire formed in her right palm. Cupping it between her hands, Taranee focused hard.

The fireball began to grow.

It expanded outward like a slowly inflating beach ball. As it did, Taranee couldn't help admiring her handiwork.

"Guys!"

Taranee was jolted out of her moment of self-praise by the sound of Hay Lin's voice.

"Take a look at what I found," Hay Lin cried out from her position in the corner. "It's Elyon's crown!"

"Don't touch that!" Cedric bellowed.

Oh! Taranee thought. Now it looks like it's Hay Lin who's in the hot spot!

Cedric began to move toward Hay Lin. Urging her fireball to grow faster, Taranee hurried after him. Through Cedric's buggy legs – each one about dozen feet long – she could just see Hay Lin. The air Guardian was hovering next to an ornate chest. A bright light spilled from the trunk, bathing Hay Lin in a warm glow. Hay Lin looked strong and defiant as she stood between Cedric and the Crown of Light.

Her fingers began to creep toward the trunk.

"I won't tell you again, Guardian," Cedric

roared. "Get away from there."

"Done deal, Cedric," Hay Lin retorted. "But do you mind if I take a little souvenir with me?"

Quick as a dragonfly, Hay Lin snatched up the Crown of Light. Taranee gasped. Here in the gloom of the abyss, the crown's gleam was even more dazzling than it had been the first time Taranee had seen it.

That had been when Phobos had placed it on the head of Elyon's astral drop in his first attempt to murder the young princess.

Taranee's thoughts turned to the battle raging above them. Who knows if he's succeeded now? she wondered, glancing up at the ceiling fearfully. We've got to find out, ASAP, which means we've *got* to get out of here – *with* that crown!

Hay Lin was off to a good start. As Cedric roared and took another swipe at her, she took flight. She swooped over his head, disorienting him with a flash of shimmery wings and long, blue-black pigtails.

"I've got the crown, guys," she called to her friends.

"Yes!" Taranee yelled.

"You shouldn't have done that!" Cedric

countered threateningly. Gasping and snarling desperately, he looked around the abyss.

Uh-oh, Taranee thought. He's looking for targets, and he's got only four choices – Cornelia, Will, Irma, or me!

"Cedric!"

Taranee jumped when a strange voice bellowed out of the darkness. I guess I left someone out, she thought; but who?

A sudden burst of light in the centre of the room answered Taranee's question. Standing in the middle of the blinding glow was an apparition – a translucent astral projection of Prince Phobos.

"Your Highness!" Cedric sputtered, bowing his head toward the prince's image.

"Elyon has been defeated," Phobos announced. "Rid yourself of those foolish girls, and bring my crown to me immediately."

Taranee's heart lurched. Defeated? She thought. Not Elyon! Has my worst fear come true? Could she really be gone?

Taranee didn't know. All she could do was hope that Phobos was lying, as he had done so many times in the past.

One thing, though, she did know.

Cedric was squirming.

"I . . . er . . ." he stuttered.

Phobos gave Cedric a hard stare. It gave Taranee, the fire Guardian, a chill.

Cedric had no choice but to say, "At once, sire!"

Phobos disappeared, and Cedric turned to face the girls. Hay Lin had landed by then. Her friends crowded around her protectively.

"Did you hear that?" Cedric said, taking a step toward the girls and trying to sound brave. "The prince has destroyed your friend, and now you're going to join her!"

"If that worm hurt Elyon," Cornelia sputtered, "I swear, I – "

Will grabbed Cornelia's arm before she could get too close to Cedric. "Calm down, Cornelia," she warned. "He's just trying to scare us."

But when Will turned to whisper something to Taranee, it was clear that Cedric's ploy had worked. Will *was* scared.

"Taranee," she whispered urgently. "Do you think you could manage to contact Elyon? We absolutely must find out how she is!"

Taranee let her fireball evaporate in a wisp

of smoke. At that point, her ability to communicate with her friends without speaking a word was *way* more important than her firepower.

"I'll try," she promised Will. "I'll use all of my telepathic powers."

"Great!" Will whispered breathlessly. "In the meantime, we'll keep Cedric occupied."

"Come on, guys!" Irma agreed. She'd been eavesdropping, as usual. Now she was linking arms with Will and moving closer to Cedric. Cornelia joined them, and Hay Lin stood just behind the trio, clutching the crown.

With all of those distractions in place, Taranee darted toward another of the abyss's shadowy corners.

Putting her fingertips to her temples, she squeezed her eyes shut. She tried to relax, to clear her mind and concentrate on producing a telepathic channel.

"Raaarrgggh!" Cedric roared, behind her.

"What's the matter," Irma taunted, "you don't like seawater in your ears?"

Okay, Taranee thought as her eyes involuntarily fluttered open, clearing my mind is obviously not going to happen right now.

But she *had* to give it her best shot. Taranee

willed her eyes closed once more. She scrunched up her face until suddenly it struck her: she knew what to do!

Taranee pictured Elyon's face.

She imagined Elyon's pale, freckled skin and pointy chin. She pictured her long, straw-coloured braids and her Metamoorian gown. She even imagined Elyon's frightened, pale-blue eyes.

Elyon, Taranee called out mentally. She searched the murky, cosmic space that linked her with her friends and called Elyon's name over and over.

Elyon she wailed.

Elyon! Elyon Brown.

Taranee waited for a response – a word, a groan, *some* sign that Elyon could hear her.

She heard nothing.

Feeling panic begin to well up inside, Taranee focused harder. She refused to believe that Phobos had succeeded this time. He couldn't have struck Elyon down. He just *couldn't* have.

Elyon! Taranee screamed silently. *Elyon, where are you?*

TEN

Elyon moaned as her eyes fluttered open.

At least, she *thought* they'd opened. It was hard to tell, because she couldn't see a thing! The air around her was ink-black, heavy, and dank. It reminded her of the Heatherfield shell cave after a heavy rain.

Elyon shifted a bit, wincing as her head moved against the hard floor. The rest of her body ached, too.

Suddenly, Elyon remembered the cause of all her aches and pains. Phobos had knocked her out! She'd been sprawled on the floor for who knew how long!

The longer I lie here, she thought in terror, the more vulnerable I am. For all I know, Phobos is nearby, watching my every move, just waiting to attack.

Breathing in raspy gasps, Elyon lurched to her feet. She felt around for a wall, a chair, some surface on which to lean until she had caught her breath. But standing still wasn't a choice. Not when Phobos was still on the loose.

Elyon stifled a panicked sob and took a tentative step forward. When her foot made contact with solid ground, she took another step. And then another.

Soon, she found herself hurrying through the dark, her arms outstretched.

"Is . . . is anyone there?" she called out in the darkness. "Can anybody hear me?"

Her own voice echoed back at her. Elyon was alone. She walked on.

As she moved slowly along, Elyon felt as if she were reaching out for something specific, looking for something she'd lost.

Suddenly, she caught her breath. Up ahead, she saw a bit of brightness shining through the darkness.

"There's a light," Elyon whispered to herself. "Maybe I'm saved."

Or maybe, she thought an instant later,

that's Phobos, coming to attack.

Elyon tightened her fists and hurried toward the light, ready to take on whatever lay ahead. Only when she stepped into its warm glow was she finally able to see its source.

A beautiful woman was standing in the centre of this black nothingness, holding a bronze, blossom-shaped lantern. The woman's slender body was sheathed in an elaborate, collared gown of turquoise and light-yellow silk. An elaborate halo of brown hair cascaded over her shoulders. Elyon couldn't stop gaping at the woman's face! She had skin the colour of pale honey, a pointy chin, and wan, wide-set blue eyes, just like . . .

"But, but I know you!" Elyon suddenly cried, rushing toward the woman. "You're . . ."

"Yes, Elyon!" the woman said. "I'm your mother!"

Elyon immediately felt her throat close up. She had so many things she wanted to ask this strange – yet utterly familiar – woman. She wanted to gaze at that face for hours, comparing it to her own. She wanted to throw her arms around her mother's neck and give her a hug that lasted forever. She wanted –

"What's happened to you?" her mother said, interrupting Elyon's thoughts. Her eyes were clouded with concern.

Tears sprang to Elyon's eyes. How could her mother know how much Elyon had craved such motherly concern? She was overcome with emotion.

"I battled Phobos," Elyon whispered. "But he tricked me. He's evil!"

"Phobos is a weak man," Elyon's mother conceded. "But you must help him! He is the only family you have left."

Great, Elyon thought, feeling grief flood over her. My sole relative is a total baddie who only wants to get rid of me. Some luck!

Once again, the woman seemed to know just what Elyon needed to hear. Reaching toward her, she said softly, "Your father and I would love to be there by your side, my little one."

"I miss you so much!" Elyon wailed, crying harder now. As tears spilled down her cheeks, she reached for her mother.

Her fingers slipped right through her mother's outstretched hand, as if the woman weren't even there.

For an instant, Elyon was shocked, but all too quickly, reality set in.

Of course, she thought, covering her face with her hands as she was racked by a fresh round of sobs. She's a ghost. She's not even really here. She's my own mother and I can't even feel her hand or give her a hug or –

"Elyon!"

Elyon started. That voice – it wasn't her mother's, but it *was* definitely familiar.

"Elyon!" the voice called again.

Elyon wiped away her tears and looked around. Her mother – or her mother's apparition, anyway – had disappeared. She had been replaced by . . . Taranee!

Elyon could see her friend floating in the air high above her, looking around desperately. Elyon was directly beneath her, gazing up at the soles of her shoes, yet Taranee didn't seem to see her.

"Can you hear me?" the Guardian was calling. "Answer me, Elyon."

Have I become a ghost, too? Elyon wondered. The thought filled her with such horror that she began to scream out frantically, "Taranee! Here I am! Taranee!"

Elyon flung her arms over her head, reaching for her friend's feet. It didn't do any good. Taranee had no idea that Elyon was close by.

"Taraneeeee!" Elyon screamed.

It was useless. The harder Elyon tried to connect with Taranee, the farther away Taranee got! The faint light that illuminated her friend was becoming dimmer and dimmer. Elyon felt as if she were falling backward, tunneling down into the dark.

"Taranee," she moaned. Her head was getting fuzzy again. She could barely keep her eyes open. She blinked heavily, struggling to stay awake.

Her first attempt to move made Elyon realise why her brother had felt secure leaving her alone. She was tied up! Coils of magical white ropes bound her arms and legs.

"Taranee . . ." Elyon moaned once more.

To her shock, Taranee answered. Elyon could hear her friend's voice loud and clear now. Elyon looked around the throne hall for her friend. She was confused when she saw that the room was empty.

Don't speak out loud, Taranee silently admonished her. *I'm contacting you mentally.*

Answer by thinking really hard. How are you?

Elyon hesitated for only one bewildered instant. Then she did as Taranee had ordered.

Phobos is holding me prisoner, she thought in reply. *He knocked me out, but I think I'm still in one piece.*

That's good news! Taranee responded almost immediately.

It had worked! Taranee had heard her. Elyon wasn't alone anymore! She listened closely as Taranee gave her an update on the situation.

We're battling Cedric, Taranee reported, *and Hay Lin just got the Crown of Light!*

Good going! Elyon responded. *Without that, Phobos can't do anything to harm me!*

Right, Taranee replied. *We just have one problem. Cedric has no intention of letting us take the crown out of here!*

ELEVEN

Back in the Abyss of Shadows, Will was glaring up at Cedric as she blasted him with bright pink force. On either side of her, Irma and Cornelia were concentrating on bombarding him with all of their magic strength as well.

Will gave each of her friends a quick, encouraging smile. "Just keep the magic coming," she whispered to them, "and we'll be okay."

Will glanced back into the dark corner where Taranee had been hiding while she tried to contact Elyon.

I wonder if she's been able to reach her yet, Will thought.

Then she returned her attention to Cedric, thrusting her palm toward him.

She took careful aim and shot a flash of pink light right into his horrible black eyes!

"Raaaarrrggggh!" the creature cried. He raked his craggy claws over his face.

Here's my opportunity! Will thought. Spinning around, she ran over to Taranee's corner. Taranee was just pulling her index fingers away from her temples.

"Well?" Will asked breathlessly.

"Everything's okay!" Taranee announced. "Elyon is still alive, but now she's Phobos's prisoner. She fainted when he hit her on the head. But she's not defeated. Phobos wants her alive, at least until he gets his hands on the crown!"

Will gave Taranee an encouraging thumbs-up before turning back to the battle.

Boy, she thought. I finally understand what my mum means when she talks about multi-tasking. On top of helping my friends battle this big, buggy bully, I've got to protect the Crown of Light *and* figure out a plan to defeat Phobos. But before we can do any of that, we've got to get Cedric out of the way.

Cornelia and Irma were currently doing their best to accomplish just that, pummeling Cedric with every bit of magic ammo they had.

But nothing seemed to be enough to conquer the nasty villain completely. Every time he recovered from one of their blows he scanned the abyss hungrily, stopping only when his eyes landed on Hay Lin.

And the Crown of Light she was clutching in her hands.

The crown! Will thought. I've got a feeling that's both our problem and our solution! Without that crown, Phobos can't win. On the other hand, our having it isn't helping us get out of this situation.

As Will pondered that quandary, Cedric began to lumber toward Hay Lin. Will put her brainstorming on pause to conjure up a ball of magic and lob it at the giant bug.

"Raaaarrggggh!" he screamed again. In retaliation for Will's attack, the confused beast slashed at Hay Lin with his fist. She ducked out of the way just in time! Cedric managed only to punch a deep hole into the room's stone wall.

Once she saw that Hay Lin was okay, Will turned her thoughts to the crown. The spell cast on the crown would be deadly to Elyon. But if the spell were broken before Elyon placed it on her head . . .

Suddenly, Will gasped. "I'm so dumb!" she exclaimed. "Why didn't I think of it before?"

While Cornelia, Irma, and Taranee continued to keep Cedric at bay, Will ran to Hay Lin and grabbed the Crown of Light out of her hands.

"Huh?" Hay Lin blurted out in confusion. "Wait, Will!"

Will couldn't afford to wait. If she waited, she might begin to reconsider the plan she was about to launch – and it was the only plan she had!

Come on, you can do this, Will urged herself. You've got the Heart of Candracar in you! And you've come this far, haven't you?

She stepped out in front of her friends and put a sudden stop to their magical assault on the monster. She looked Cedric right in his stony, black eyes and declared, "Enough fighting, Cedric. You want the crown? Take it!"

The other Guardians gasped.

Cedric looked dubious.

"So, you're giving up, are you?" he asked, uncertainly.

Will felt Cornelia's fingers squeezing her shoulder hard.

"What do you think you're doing?" Cornelia

whispered in Will's ear. "You don't really want to give him the crown, do you?"

"I'm not crazy, Cornelia," Will whispered back. "Trust me."

Cornelia's hand slid away. She stepped back to join Taranee, Irma, and Hay Lin. Will smiled over her shoulder. Having her own wall of friends behind her made her feel a little braver.

Just a little.

I hope I've got the right idea, she thought again, biting her lip anxiously.

Cedric was growing impatient. He moved toward her.

"The crown, Will," he rasped.

"Sure, Cedric," Will responded with a glare. "Come and get it!"

The giant creature slouched over.

That's it, Will thought. Come a little closer, Cedric.

And he did, reaching greedily for the crown.

When Will was close enough to see the intricate markings on the monster's scaly skin, she made her move. Flinging out her arm, she hit Cedric with the biggest blast of magic she'd ever created!

"Brawwwwww!" the monster shrieked as he

fell backward at the force of the blow. He landed in a heap on the floor, breathing heavily.

"You underhanded little wretch," Cedric spat at Will. "You're not fighting fair!"

Oh, *that's* rich, Will thought. Cedric talking about fighting fair. Just a few of the many horrible things Cedric had done flashed through Will's mind. She remembered how he'd deceived Elyon into coming to Metamoor, then turned her against her friends.

He'd helped kidnap Taranee and had imprisoned her deep within the palace for weeks.

He'd lied. Cheated. Destroyed.

Except that now, Will thought, he's done those things for the last time. I'll make sure of that.

She began to sprint toward the fallen creature. The closer she got to him, the more grotesque he looked. Will's stomach churned. Only the thought of her friends – especially Elyon – urged her on.

Using all the strength in her long legs, Will took a flying leap – and landed right on Cedric's back! She scrambled up the monster's knobby spine until she was straddling his ridged neck.

Grabbing the crown with both hands, she slapped it onto Cedric's head.

Screaming in shock, Cedric began to flail and buck, but Will held on tight.

"Don't talk to *me* about fair," she grunted, pushing the crown further down on Cedric's head. "You don't set a very good example yourself."

Cedric could only respond with a horrible shriek of pain. His head rolled back and forth and then began thrashing violently.

Cedric arched backward. Will took the opportunity to loosen her grip on the creature's neck and hop to the floor.

"*YAAAARRRGGGH!*" Cedric let out another shriek as Will darted out of his way.

"I did it!" Will exclaimed, running to her friends.

"Yeah," Irma agreed, watching in horror as Cedric writhed on the floor. "But . . . what did you do?"

"That crown absorbs powers," Will pointed out proudly. "So I thought, if it worked on Elyon's astral drop, why shouldn't it work on Cedric, too?"

"Oh, my gosh!" Taranee squeaked. "Look!"

Will and the other Guardians followed Taranee's gaze to Cedric. They gasped in unison.

The big red monster that had been terrorising them a moment ago was gone. Cedric was morphing.

His face was taking on a more human shape. Then it morphed yet again, and a pulpy red mask appeared over his eyes. His chin elongated itself until it came to a menacing point. His legs fused together into a green, slimy tail.

When his transformation was complete, Cedric uttered one woozy "oooh," before collapsing in a heap.

He was out cold.

"Good thinking, Will!" Taranee exclaimed. She tiptoed closer to Cedric to take a closer look. "Cedric went back to his true form."

"Yeah," Hay Lin said, giving Cedric's body a glare. "Back to the snake he is."

"Even better," Cornelia added, "the big bully is out cold."

"But it's not over yet," Will reminded her friends. She pointed at the crown, which had bounced off Cedric's head when he'd hit the ground. The platinum headpiece continued to glow, and its bright purple central stone pulsated brilliantly.

"The crown is still protected by the spell," Will said, "and there's only one way to destroy it."

Will hurried over to the crown and scooped it up. She brought it back to her friends. The Guardians clustered around their leader.

Standing in the centre of their circle, Will held on to the crown. To her amazement, her stomach was fluttering, not with fear, but with excitement. For the first time since beginning her Guardian gig, Will felt sure of her decision.

She also had complete faith in her friends.

"Focus your power as never before," she ordered them. "The Heart of Candracar has already defeated Phobos's energy. Now we'll let it do the same thing to the Crown of Light. *Right* now!"

Will wrapped her right hand around the crown. One after another, each of her friends also gripped a section.

When everyone was holding on, Will closed her eyes and concentrated. She thought of Elyon, sitting tied up in the palace. She thought of Metamoor, released from its dark gloom. Finally, she thought of her mother, at home in Heatherfield, happy and safe from the Metamoorian invaders that she didn't even know existed.

Will squeezed her eyes shut, willing the curse away from the Crown of Light.

Slowly but surely, something started to happen! Even through her closed eyelids, Will could see a blinding white light emanating from the crown.

She could feel it, too.

"Ah!" Irma suddenly cried. "The crown is burning hot!"

"Don't let go!" Will said. "Come on! We can do it! We can do it!"

Fwoooooommm!

As if to prove this point, the girls suddenly began rising together into the air. Will opened her eyes and glanced beneath her. The Guardians were being lifted up by a bubble of magic that flashed and pulsated around them. Its colour was the same as that of Will's magic – a vivid, beautiful pink.

"Yes!" Will cried out. "It's working! *Heart of Candracar, forever break this curse, free this crown and protect those who wear it!*"

TWELVE

Elyon was still bound by magic ropes, but she was no longer alone.

Phobos had returned. He sat on his ridiculously ornate throne, waiting with his sister for news from the Abyss of Shadows. Phobos looked jumpy, eager – ready for a fight.

Well, he's going to get one, Elyon thought sullenly. He's just waiting for his prize, the Crown of Light. Like the Guardians are going to let *that* happen, she thought with a little snort. There's no way!

Right?

Elyon had to admit that all of the mysterious booms and roars echoing from beneath the floor *were* making her a little nervous. What was going on down there? She couldn't take much more waiting around for answers. She needed to know what was happening.

Brrrrrmmmmmrrrrrr!

Elyon gasped. It sounded as though she were about to get her wish. The floor had suddenly started trembling. Elyon looked up. For a moment, her eyes met those of her brother: the pale blue irises; the slightly sleepy cast to the upper lids; the long, light eyelashes . . . gazing at Phobos's face was like looking in a mirror.

And it filled Elyon with disgust. She looked down at her hands, desperate to separate herself from her evil brother, to somehow rise above him –

"Huh?" Elyon suddenly gasped.

Her wish had come true – literally! Elyon was rising into the air! She had been caught up somehow inside a giant bubble of golden light. Now she was floating high above her befuddled brother.

"What?" Phobos barked, jumping to his feet to glare at her. "Now what's happening?"

"I think I can tell you, Phobos, but you might not be very happy with the answer," Elyon replied. She started to tell Phobos what she knew in her heart – that the Guardians had won their battle with Cedric. They had the Crown of Light, and now they were coming to Elyon's rescue.

But before Elyon could tell him all that, he learned it for himself.

Way below her floating feet, the green mosaic on the palace floor went liquid once again. With a hot *hssssssss*, they began to melt together, forming a soft, permeable substance. And a moment later, a giant, clear orb rose into the throne hall. Standing inside the bubble were the five Guardians. Each glared out of the sphere with an expression of stony determination.

At the girls' feet lay Cedric – unconscious.

"Oh, no-o-o-o-o!" Phobos wailed. He jumped to his feet and stared at the girls in utter shock.

"Oh, yes, Phobos," Will spat back.

"This must be yours," Irma added. She gave Cedric a mighty shove with her purple boot, causing him to fall out of the orb and hit the tiles with a sick *splat*. The impact startled him awake. The bubble burst, and the five Guardians dropped lightly to the floor.

"Cedric!" Phobos shrieked. While he looked in horror at his defeated soldier, Elyon grinned at the Guardians.

"Guys," she said softly. "Am I glad to see you!"

"Unnhhh."

Cedric was groaning at the sound of his master's rage.

"Sire," Cedric stuttered, "I – "

"Silence, incompetent fool," Phobos bellowed. "You weren't even remotely capable of destroying the Guardians, so I shall have to deal with them myself!"

Phobos whirled to face Elyon's friends. "Your time has come, Guardians," Phobos cried. "Are you ready?"

"No, Phobos!" Will declared. "We won't fight you. That's up to the new queen of Meridian!"

It took Elyon a moment to realise that Will was talking about *her*. She looked over at the leader of the Guardians.

Will was holding the Crown of Light. It twinkled in her hand like a fallen comet. Its power lifted Will straight into the air – and brought her right to Elyon.

She held the crown above Elyon's head.

"Go on, Elyon," she whispered with a reassuring smile. "Show him who you are!" Will reached out to place the crown atop her friend's head gently.

"I . . ." Elyon started to protest. But the moment the crown settled comfortably onto her head, something amazing happened. Elyon felt something she'd never experienced before. She was literally filled with light! Her insides felt airy, and her skin shone, casting off a gentle blue glow.

Elyon felt the magic ropes that bound her suddenly become solid, then crack into a dozen pieces. As her bindings tumbled to the floor, she felt truly free, perhaps for the first time in her life. Elyon and the crown were united in a wave of pure and absolute power.

Still floating, Elyon looked down. Reflecting her inner light back at her, the room went from grey and shadowy to sparkling and pearly.

The darkness is dissolving, Elyon said to herself in wonder. A new day is beginning. It's what Phobos has always feared, and what the people of Metamoor have always hoped for – the Light of Meridian is returning to shine once again. The Light of Meridian. The Light of Meridian is me! And never again will anyone stop the splendor of this magic – this power!

Not even, Elyon thought darkly, my brother, Phobos.

Elyon floated down toward the floor. When she landed, she regarded the prince. He was sprawled on the floor, apparently emptied of all power. His face was pale, and his lips were stretched in a tight line.

"Go ahead, little sister," he spat. "I'm not afraid. Do what you must."

He thinks I'm going to kill him, Elyon thought, because that is exactly what he would have done to me!

Instead, Elyon pointed at her brother with a royal finger. "For all the pain you've inflicted, the people of Meridian and I want only one thing," Elyon declared to the prince. "To forget all about you!"

With one wave of her glowing hand, she conjured up two new sets of magical ropes. The coils snaked their way around Phobos and Cedric, immobilizing them completely.

When Elyon turned to flash her friends a triumphant smile, they gazed back at her in awe.

"Can we hug you?" Cornelia asked, laughing. "Or would a bow be more appropriate?"

Elyon giggled. "Don't make me laugh," she said to her old friend. "I'm true royalty now. I'm glowing with the Light of Meridian. So I have to maintain *proper* decorum."

The Guardians dissolved into even more giggles.

Elyon was so immersed in this moment of simple happiness she didn't notice Irma creeping up to the hole in the wall of the palace. When Irma peeked out – and gasped in shock – Elyon's heart sank.

I should have known our peace would be short-lived, she thought. What now?

"Maybe you should take a look down there," Irma said to Elyon in a small voice.

Elyon walked over to the hole. As she peeked through, she couldn't help noticing the shafts of silver-blue light she was involuntarily sending out into the grey air! Her very presence seemed to weaken the city's gloom, giving the sky a little extra sparkle, the trees an extra dose of green, and the people a bit of rosiness in their cheeks.

Speaking of people . . .

"There are thousands of them," Elyon whispered to her friends. "Look at the crowd that's gathered!"

The area around the castle – just beyond the thicket of poisonous black roses – was teeming with Metamoorians. Countless green, orange, and blue faces were all looking hopefully toward Elyon.

"There she is," one woman shouted as she spotted the queen. "It's Elyon!"

"Elyon!" echoed a few more people.

"The princess has won!" shouted another voice from the crowd. "Phobos is defeated!"

"Long live the new ruler of Meridian! Elyon!"

Elyon was completely overwhelmed. Being queen among her closest friends was easy. But dealing with masses of needy subjects was another thing entirely!

"Look at them!" Elyon gulped to her friends. "What . . . what do I do now?"

"I'm no expert in coronations," Will responded, "but I think you say something to them."

"Elyon, you're their queen now," Cornelia pointed out. Her eyes filled up with pride.

"Queen?" Elyon whispered. Hearing the word made everything seem much more official. "I'm not sure I'm ready for this."

"Sure you are," Irma said, giving Elyon's incandescent shoulder a little push. "Go on, queenie!"

Elyon gazed down at the people.

My people, she realised suddenly.

Then, just as suddenly, her doubts disappeared. A sense of peace and wisdom flooded Elyon's mind. She knew just what to do.

Rising from the ground, she floated through the rough hole in the castle wall and down toward the crowd. Hovering above the hedge of poisonous roses, she began to speak.

"Friends," she called out. She was not surprised to find her voice amplified so that it echoed through the crowd. "People of Meridian. My brother's reign is finished forever, and I . . . I want to ask your forgiveness for everything you've undergone."

Elyon spotted Vathek on the ground just below. He was nodding and smiling in approval.

Smiling back at him, Elyon floated down to the weedy, parched grass just beyond the black roses. "Forgiveness is an act of generosity," Elyon continued, addressing her people. "So I've decided to share something with you, too. Something that belongs to me but which I don't deserve. There was a time when a magical force flowed through this land. And so, I call upon my powers to make it flow once again!"

Elyon lifted both arms into the air.

Kwaaammmm!

The power that sprang from Elyon's body shook the city of Meridian. But unlike the violent jolts of the recent battle, this magic felt like a *whoosh* of warmth. It emanated in circles from the queen. In its wake, the grass became greener. Wildflowers sprang up from once-arid dirt. Birds began twittering in the once-barren trees.

Vathek crouched to place one blue claw upon the grass. "The ground is heating up!" he exclaimed.

Elyon smiled. Somehow, she had known that that would happen.

"May evil disappear from this world!" she proclaimed. "May every spell cast by Phobos be removed! May Meridian spring back to life!"

Elyon threw her head back, unleashing

another burst of magic. Great swirls of silver-blue magic shot upward, piercing the sky's shroud of grey.

Brilliant sunlight poured through the clouds. It skimmed over the crowd, filling the emptiness in the citizens' hearts with pure, positive energy. Then it began to weave its way through the hedge of black roses, caressing each bloom lovingly.

Instantly, the black flowers began to be transformed. Where petals had been, long hair appeared. The roses' centres became faces with sleepy red eyes and colourful cheeks. The walls of the flowery cage were bursting open, and its prisoners were being set free!

Elyon spotted two former flowers in particular that looked oddly familiar, as if she had seen them before – a mother and daughter with green skin, pointy ears, and apple-red eye masks. The two former flowers were searching the grounds for someone – someone who suddenly pushed through the crowd with a choked cry of joy.

"Daltar!" the woman cried.

"Daddy!" the little girl squealed.

It was Daltar's wife and daughter – the very

first to have been changed by Phobos into black blooms. Their release meant that Meridian really was coming back to life!

It was becoming a place where Elyon felt – at long last – at home.

But now it was time to say goodbye to those whose home was elsewhere.

After stopping briefly to say hello to Vathek, Elyon waved to her subjects and floated back up to the palace, where her friends waited. Still glowing brightly, she landed between the Guardians and her brother. Phobos had already abandoned his cocky stoicism and was squirming inside his bonds.

"Ah!" he scolded. "All that power, wasted on those worthless wretches. You're just a foolish little girl."

"Yes, Phobos," she said in a lilting voice. "I'm a foolish girl who's finally happy!"

"Yeah!" Hay Lin said. "You just don't get it, Phobos. My grandmother used to tell me a Tibetan saying: 'If you don't understand your punishment, you deserve another one!'"

Elyon turned her back on her brother. Her enemy wasn't nearly as important as her friends – especially . . .

"Cornelia," Elyon said softly. She cupped an object that Vathek had given her a moment ago, when she had stopped to speak to him – a beautiful white lily, glowing as brightly as Elyon's own hands. It was Caleb, Cornelia's love, who had been transformed forever into a flower. "This is for you," Elyon said. "It's from Vathek."

"Oh," Cornelia said. Her eyes went teary, this time with grief. Still, she managed to give Elyon a grateful smile.

Elyon smiled back at her and then at all her friends.

"I just don't know what to say to you all," she said. "Without you, none of this would have been possible!"

"We only did what had to be done," Will said.

"And now, can you come back to Heatherfield?" Cornelia asked. Elyon looked at her friend's pale, beautiful face.

"I don't think I will be going back, Cornelia," Elyon admitted gently. "This is my world now. But you'll come back to see me, won't you?"

A brief flash of pain clouded Cornelia's face,

but then she smiled. "You can count on it," she declared. "But – hey, what's happening?"

Elyon bit her lip. *She* knew exactly what was happening.

With acceptance comes peace, she thought, and with peace comes a journey to the place where one belongs. For my friends, that place is not Meridian.

The Guardians became shimmery and translucent.

They were fading away, before Elyon's very eyes.

They were going home, and Elyon was staying behind. Metamoor was her destiny and – she hoped – her everlasting joy.

THIRTEEN

In the destroyed throne hall of Phobos's palace, Hay Lin couldn't stop staring. Elyon was beautiful with the Crown of Light upon her head. She really did seem to glow from within.

When goodness comes to life, Hay Lin realised in awe, this is what it must look like. Like an angel or fairy or magic nymph!

Hay Lin glanced over her shoulder at Cedric and Phobos, who were crouched in the shadows of the furthest corners of the room, still growling and struggling against their magic bindings.

We won, Hay Lin realised. We beat them! Well, Elyon did, really. But we helped! Now it's time to celebrate! Since planning parties is totally my area of expertise, I can help

Elyon throw a big bash, with tons of food and music and decor –

"Hey," Cornelia suddenly piped up. "What's happening?"

Hay Lin glanced at her friend – and gasped!

Cornelia was . . . she was transparent! Her eyes grew wider as she began to fade away.

She wasn't the only one, either. Will was looking ghostly, and Irma was positively see-through. Taranee wasn't all there, either.

Which, Hay Lin thought with a gulp, can only mean . . .

Hay Lin held her own hands up before her face. Yup! They looked as if they were made of cellophane. Hay Lin felt her friends' eyes on her.

"Don't look at me!" she protested. "I didn't touch anything."

She clearly couldn't remedy this problem, either. The girls were fading fast. Hay Lin took one last, desperate look at Elyon.

Through the silver-blue glow that haloed her face, Elyon was smiling reassuringly and waving goodbye to her friends.

One adventure ends, Hay Lin thought, and another begins. I just hope the next one is *slightly* less scary than the last few we've gone on. I'm ready for a little bit of a break!

As the Guardians began to shimmer into nothingness, Irma complained, "Everything can't just disappear like this! I didn't get my hero's acclaim! I didn't get to sign a single autograph!"

Schwoooooommm!

There was no time to protest any further. The girls found themselves in a white and airy room. They clustered together and nervously looked around.

"Huh?" Irma blurted. "Where are we?"

And what, Hay Lin wondered in irritation, are *they* doing here?

She was glaring over her shoulder at Cedric and Phobos. The prisoners had somehow made the journey with them!

Where have we landed? Hay Lin thought.

Looking around, Hay Lin knew only one thing: the Guardians had definitely come to a good place – a breathtakingly gorgeous place! The whiteness was then replaced by the most stunning sight Hay Lin had ever seen. It was a vast, circular room with a floor inlaid with pink marble, silver granite, and tiles of onyx, amethyst, emerald, and sapphire. Its starburst design was so intricate Hay Lin couldn't believe it had been shaped by human hands.

When she tore her eyes from the incredible artwork and looked around the rest of the hall, she gasped.

I should have known, she thought. This mosaic *wasn't* shaped by human hands.

Looking around the domed room, she saw a dozen giant thrones, each decorated with its own amazing artwork. In each of the chairs sat a strange creature.

One had flaps like giant rabbit's ears jutting out of its head. Another had a wolfish face and a long, blue mane. Another was bright pink! He looked as gentle and soft as a tamed bear.

All of these exotic strangers, in fact, wore welcoming, kind expressions, and were bathed in a pink-gold sunlight that flooded in through the windows –

Oh, my gosh, Hay Lin thought with another gasp.

The windows!

The glassless, dramatically arched window frames were just as beautiful as everything else in the strange hall. But that wasn't what was making Hay Lin wide-eyed and breathless.

It was the view, or lack of one, through the windows that stunned her.

There were no trees, no mountains, no streets, no other buildings. Just impossibly brilliant sunshine, and lots and lots of white, puffy clouds.

Somehow, Hay Lin realised, we're in a place in the middle of the sky. But how is that possible? And why have we been brought here? And –

"You have completed your task, Guardians."

Hay Lin's musings were interrupted by two people who'd just entered the grand, circular room. One was a young man with a pale, hairless head and a kind smile. He was floating several feet above the floor, propelled forward by nothing more than magical impulse.

Directly behind this stranger plodded a much older man. He was swathed in flowing robes and had a white beard that almost reached his ankles.

"Welcome," the younger man said. The single word made Hay Lin swoon. The man's voice was gentle and soothing.

"Welcome," he said again, "to Candracar!"

"C – C – Candracar?" Hay Lin sputtered. "*The* Candracar?"

"Do you know of any other?" the older man said with a smile in his wise eyes.

"Nice going," Irma whispered as Hay Lin's cheeks grew hot with embarrassment. "As always, you've made a great first impression."

The man waved Irma's comment away. Clearly, she hadn't whispered softly enough!

Or maybe, Hay Lin realised breathlessly, he's psychic. Maybe this is –

"I am the Oracle," the man confirmed, winking at Hay Lin once again. "And I am very pleased finally to greet you in Candracar!"

"Not too shabby," Irma whispered.

Hay Lin had to agree. This place was about as far from shabby as Hay Lin could ever have imagined. She wanted to remember every detail of it – the amazing, sparkly quality of the light; the wonderfully weird beings inhabiting the room.

"The Congregation," the older man rumbled, motioning toward the beings in the giant thrones, "pays you its highest honours!"

"One of its members in particular," the

Oracle added, "is very happy to see you."

"Hello, sweetheart!"

The voice – thin and reedy, yet strong and sweet – came from just behind Hay Lin.

She froze.

Then, she burst into tears of joy.

"Grandma?" she squeaked happily.

Almost afraid to break the spell, Hay Lin peeked over her shoulder.

More tears sprang from her eyes, and she let out another squeal of joy.

Her grandmother – the woman who'd been Hay Lin's mentor and best friend, who'd launched Hay Lin into this crazy new life – was actually standing right there in front of her.

And this wasn't a transparent ghost or talking hologram – Hay Lin just knew it! This really was her grandmother, in the flesh.

Hay Lin threw herself into the elder Guardian's open arms. "Grandma!" she sobbed.

"Hello, Hay Lin," the old woman whispered. Just as it always had, her long, silver hair felt like silk. She smelled like jasmine oil. Her hug was strong and sweet, and its comfort had a ripple effect. As Hay Lin luxuriated in her grandmother's embrace, she caught the sound of several sniffles behind her.

"Anyone have a tissue, by any chance?" she heard Irma gulp.

"I – I'm afraid not," came Will's choked voice.

Giggling through her own tears, Hay Lin finally pulled herself away from her grandmother – though not too far away. She wrapped one arm around the tiny lady's shoulders, then turned to her friends. They, too, had an amazing connection to Hay Lin's grandmother. It was she who had told all five girls of their powers. So it wasn't fair of Hay Lin to hog all the hugging.

"Come here, girls," Yan Lin beckoned.

Wiping away their tears, the Guardians stepped forward.

"You were just wonderful," Yan Lin exclaimed. "I'm so proud of you all!"

"Does that mean . . . our mission is over?" Will asked in a quivery voice.

Hay Lin held her breath.

On one hand, she'd savoured these magical months more than anything that had ever happened to her.

On the other hand, she'd reached her limit! Saving the earth and Metamoor; restoring Elyon to the throne; closing the portals; trying to keep her magical abilities a secret from Heatherfield's ordinary mortals – it was all too much!

So Hay Lin almost broke into more sobs – of relief this time – when Yan Lin nodded at Will.

"Yes, your mission is over," she confirmed. "With the best possible outcome."

Hay Lin looked over at the Oracle and saw that he was now walking instead of floating. He'd left the elderly man behind to come over and speak to the Guardians.

"The task entrusted to you was not the easiest of missions," he admitted. "But you outdid yourselves. Not only did you defend the Veil, you also helped bring Metamoor back to life and defeat its persecutor."

The Oracle motioned, with a disapproving eye, toward Phobos. The prince was still kneeling on the floor. His face was defiant despite his supplicant position and the magical vines that bound him.

"Punish me if you like," he scowled at the Oracle. "I will return to take my place, and, come that day, there will be no chance for your survival."

The Oracle did not reply. Phobos's slurs rolled off him like a stream of water skimming over a smooth stone. He pointed at Phobos. Immediately, two of the members of the Congregation descended from their thrones and walked over to the fallen prince. Flanking Phobos and Cedric, the congregants waited for the Oracle's order.

"May they be exiled to the Tower of Mists! They will remain there until their hearts harbour serenity!"

"I guess," Hay Lin whispered, "we won't be seeing them for a long time, then."

Once again, the Oracle had heard Hay Lin. "Phobos and Cedric are no longer your problem," he assured her. "They are in the custody of Candracar, now."

The Oracle waved his hand at the prisoners.

"Ah!" Hay Lin cried out in surprise at what she saw.

Where Phobos and Cedric sat, there was now a burst of brilliant, bright yellow light. It dazzled Hay Lin, making her literally see stars.

By the time the little sparkles in her eyes

had faded, the two evildoers were gone!

Hay Lin's friends let out exclamations of awe, too. Will gazed at the Oracle and shook her head.

"I've thought about this place a lot," she admitted. "All the time! But I never imagined it looking like this!"

The Oracle smiled kindly. Returning to his position in front of the bearded old sage, he said, "I suppose you have endless questions, don't you? What is the first thing you would like to know?"

"That guy next to you," Irma piped up. "Is he Santa Claus?"

"I beg your pardon!" the old man sputtered, obviously unprepared for Irma's jokes.

Hay Lin snorted, then clapped a hand over Irma's mouth as Taranee tightly held Irma by the shoulders.

"Um, don't mind her," Hay Lin cried to the old man. "There are just so many things we'd like to know we're not sure where to start!"

"There is a time for everything," the Oracle confirmed. "This is a time for questions, but the time for answers has not yet arrived."

Irma took a frustrated little hop and

screwed her face into a scowl. Hay Lin could just imagine what her hotheaded friend would be saying – if Hay Lin's hand hadn't been still firmly clamped over her mouth.

"If *this* isn't a time for answers, what is?" Irma would shout. "This is the end of our mission, isn't it?"

Or is it? Hay Lin wondered, feeling a chill skitter through her. Now that Metamoor is saved, I wonder what's next!

Reading her mind once again, the Oracle spoke. "Even if your mission is over," he told the girls, "you will continue to be our Guardians, and you will have the power to find the answers to everything on your own."

Hay Lin didn't know whether to jump with excitement or slump over in weariness.

More mysteries to unravel, she thought. More time waiting for the next bad guy to pop through a portal. More dodging of major disasters!

But, Hay Lin reminded herself, this also means more magic! More cool moments. And more bonding with my fellow Guardians.

She was daunted and delighted all at once.

Will, too, was clearly struggling to contain

her emotions. As the Oracle turned to leave the hall, she waved at him desperately.

"But, sir . . ." she squeaked weakly.

The Oracle only smiled again and then began to float out of the grand hall.

Like Hay Lin's grandmother, who had always doled information out to the Guardians in mysterious tidbits, the Oracle seemed intent on keeping the girls guessing.

When he had gone, his elderly attendant took over.

"We may be asking for your help again in the future," he told the Guardians. "Be vigilant, and heed every call. Your powers will serve to defend your world and all of the worlds under the watchful eye of the Oracle of Candracar."

As the old man intoned those words, Hay Lin gazed at her grandmother. The old woman was smiling contentedly, patting her granddaughter on the arm as if Hay Lin had just gotten an interesting assignment at school.

But this is huge! This is gigantic! Hay Lin thought. This means that W.I.T.C.H. isn't on some finite mission to close portals or keep track of a kidnapped friend. We're facing ongoing Guardianship of the world!

She waited for panic to start simmering within her. She braced herself for heart palpitations, sweaty palms, shortened breaths – the whole nine yards.

But instead, she felt fine. She was even a little elated.

Surprised, Hay Lin glanced at her girlfriends. None of them seemed to be freaking out, either! Their faces were animated, determined, and excited.

And suddenly, Hay Lin knew exactly why.

If I were facing this fate alone, she thought, I'd be totally overwhelmed and paralysed.

But I'm not alone.

We're not alone, Hay Lin corrected herself as she gazed at the strong and beautiful faces of Will, Irma, Taranee, and Cornelia. We're the Guardians of Candracar, we're best friends, and we're an unstoppable team. As long as we stick together, nothing can stop us from saving the world, ever!

DON'T BE SAD, GIRLS, WE'LL MEET AGAIN. THE HEART OF CANDRACAR WILL HELP YOU RETURN WHENEVER YOU WISH.

YOU ARE WELCOME HERE ANYTIME. AND CANDRACAR SERVES AS THE PASSAGEWAY TO ALL OTHER WORLDS.

GOODBYE! DON'T BE AFRAID OF WHAT LIES AHEAD.

WAIT, GRANDMA. CAN'T YOU...

IN A HEARTBEAT, IT'S ALL OVER.

...TELL US MORE?

I WASN'T EXPECTING TO SEE MY GRANDMA. AND NOW WE KNOW EVEN LESS THAN WE DID AT THE BEGINNING OF THIS WHOLE THING.

HEY, WILL, CAN YOU MAKE THE HEART OF CANDRACAR TAKE US BACK RIGHT NOW?

I THINK WE SHOULD WAIT!

WAIT? WAIT FOR **WHAT?**

DIDN'T YOU HEAR WHAT THE ORACLE SAID? IT'S NOT TIME FOR ALL THE ANSWERS.

...AND WHEN THAT TIME COMES, WE'LL BE READY!

YEAH...